THE SECRET ADVENTURES OF RAFFETY RAY

This proof is bound for your reviewing convenience.

Please check with the publisher before extracting or quoting from the text in a review.

ISBN 978 1 84898 342 7

Publication date: September 2010

Publicity and Marketing enquiries:

Matt Wilks (Marketing Manager)

Email: matt_wilks@ticktock.co.uk

Telephone: +44 (0) 1892 509400

Adam Guillain

THE SECRET ADVENTURES OF RAFFETY RAY

Illustrated by Dan Chernett

First published in Great Britain in 2010 by
TickTock Entertainment Ltd, The Old Sawmill,
103 Goods Station Road, Tunbridge Wells, Kent, TN1 2DP

ISBN: 978-1-84898-342-7

A CIP catalogue record for this book is available
from the British Library

Printed and bound in Great Britain by
CPI Antony Rowe, Chippenham and Eastbourne

for you

CONTENTS

EVIDENCE ITEM RR07
Text retrieved and decoded
from unknown computer

My name is Zap Boy and I'm fighting to save the world. It's 2038 and I'm sending you this message on my Wonder Zap-1 (there's no time to explain). You see, there are some very important things you have to know.

1. There is life on other planets.
2. Extraterrestrials are living among us.
3. Not all of them are good.

But you can help me...

CHRISTMAS EVE

The digital clock on Geek Street read 18:21 – nine minutes before curfew. Zap Boy and his faithful dog, Wham, were trudging home from school through the black snow.

'My dad said Christmas was really exciting when he was a kid,' Zap Boy moaned, taking off his glasses and giving them a wipe. 'There was this big, jolly fella called Santa living at the North Pole with thousands of elves.' Even as he said it, Zap Boy thought this sounded unlikely. The North Pole had melted like an ice lolly years ago.

'The elves made Christmas presents for boys and girls all over the world, apparently,' Zap Boy went on.

'Woof,' said Wham, not even trying to sound interested. All Wham ever got for Christmas was a squeaky bone.

'And kids could watch as much TV as they wanted – even in their bedrooms!' Zap Boy continued, putting on his specs and stuffing his freezing-cold hands deep into his pockets. 'Dad said he always got so many new toys for Christmas it would take him weeks to play with them all – and none of them had anything to do with homework *or* school!'

In Dog World, Wham was more worried about his dinner than the depressing state of children's toys. 'If it's another tin of rabbit meat, I'll die!' he snuffled, lost in his own familiar bluster. 'Beef on the other hand...' When it came to food, Wham really wished that Zap Boy understood Dog Speak.

But unfortunately for Wham, Zap Boy wasn't some kind of comic-book superhero with incredible powers. In a world where comics, computer games and toys were outlawed, Zap Boy was, for now, only real in the imagination and comic book creations of a very ordinary boy called Raffety Ray.

'I wonder what it was like around here when every flat had festive lights up at the windows?' Raffety mused. This year Prime Minister Shrub had switched off all the nation's streetlights, supposedly to save power. With so much pollution billowing out from the incinerators all over the country, the sky, like the snow, was often so black that the day sometimes seemed like night.

A blast from the horn of a passing Kutacruiser caught Zap Boy out.

'Yikes!' he cried as leapt away.

'Get a move on, Squirt!' shouted the fair-haired yob hanging out of the passenger window.

Zap Boy crashed against a wall of corrugated iron and collapsed into the snow.

'Crabite!' he cursed.

Zap Boy knew it was Konor Kram even before he saw his inanely grinning face. Kram was the only boy in school whose parents could afford an all-terrain cruiser – and boy, did he go on about it!

Wham shivered and shook out his snow-drenched coat.

'Wimp!' he growled at Raffety. 'Stand up for yourself.'

Zap Boy was about to get up when a police snowcruiser swept by.

'Seven minutes to curfew,' the policeman blurted through the megaphone on the roof. Zap Boy checked his watch.

'Better hurry, Wham boy,' he chivvied, getting up.

Zap Boy knew that he would be in Dr Braincrammer's detention for a week if he were late.

As they rushed past the boarded-up tube

station at Shepherd's Bush, the smog was fleetingly dispersed by a strong easterly wind and Zap Boy's eyes were hypnotically drawn towards a sickening sight: the massive hologram of a bushy-bearded Prime Minister Shrub, dressed in a lime-green suit and psychedelic tie. Sitting with a big cheesy grin among an array of TLC toys, Shrub's hologram loomed over the entire district.

'Toys that help you learn, help you earn,' the Prime Minister preached as his image clicked into life every ten seconds.

The Prime Minister's Thought and Learning Control Toy Company (TLC) was now the only legal toy company in the entire country, manufacturing and selling a range of 'educational' toys in line with The National Braincramming Strategy.

'Shut up!' Zap Boy sneered at Shrub's hologram.

He flinched as two CCTV cameras instantly lit up in Shrub's eyes.

Zap Boy pulled down his hood.

'I'm totally outnumbered,' sighed Raffety,

giving Zap Boy a rest. 'Even if I *had* superpowers, I couldn't fight the Prime Minister and Minister Crabwitch on my own.'

'The boy thinks big but he's got no oomph!' Wham grumbled. 'No self belief.'

As Raffety and Wham trudged on, Raffety reflected that, as terrifying as the Prime Minister was, he faded into insignificance alongside the cruel, tyrannical power wielded by Geerta Crabwitch.

Geerta Crabwitch was Minister of Child Development. Her compulsory six-day school week ran from 8:00 to 17:00 and involved daily tests and homework and an 18:30 curfew. These were just the opening rules to a never-ending list.

'*Please* don't get me anything from TLC,' Raffety had begged his dad during the run-up to Christmas. 'I'd rather have something from the Heaps.'

'You can't have second-hand toys from the dump anymore,' Mr Ray replied. 'Christmas is for new TLC toys.'

Minister Crabwitch had banned toys for

play. It was one of the thousands of rules on her list *for parents*. That's why so many great toys had been thrown away and ended up on Heaps all over the country.

'But I don't want *new* toys,' Raffety pleaded. 'TLC toys stink! They're boring, useless and...' he spooked up his voice – 'EVIL!'

'Evil?' laughed Mr Ray. 'How can toys that help you learn be evil?'

'Argh!' Raffety grunted, throwing up his hands.

Mr Ray worked for the government bank Northern Gold. To make ends meet, he moonlighted as a bin man and for years had run an on-the-side, black market business selling recycled toys. But last year's dead-of-night raids and his arrest – along with other parents like him – had changed everything.

'TLC toys help you learn – and earn more money in the future,' Mr Ray now often told his son.

'That's from the advert, darling,' Mrs Ray commented.

'Those that play, stay poor,' his dad concluded, quoting another ad.

As Raffety's mind turned to his dad, he wondered if he had been brainwashed after his arrest and was now some kind of government spy. 'Dad wouldn't have spouted claptrap like that before,' Raffety told himself.

Whatever had happened to Raffety's dad on the night of his arrest, he never spoke about it.

Raffety flinched as a roll of thunder shook the dead trees around him.

'Yuk!' he spat when a large clump of grimy snow landed – SPLAT! – on his head.

Raffety heard the whir of a CCTV camera as it turned to capture evidence of any potential crime. In a moment of madness, Raffety slipped back into Zap Boy mode, gathered a snowball and threw it straight at the lens.

ZAP!

He missed.

'ASBO,' came the robotic warning. 'This camera is recording your anti-social behaviour.'

'You goofball!' Raffety scolded himself.

In a nothing-to-lose gesture, he angrily scooped up another snowball, spun on his heels –

and slipped over before throwing it.

With Wham yapping over another ASBO from the computer, Raffety Ray fumbled through the snow for his glasses. He wiped the lenses on his coat, put them on and hauled himself up. 'I'll get detention every day for a week now,' he grumbled.

Raffety and Wham were almost home when a shiny object, lit by a brilliant white light, flashed past their dumbstruck faces and crashed into the bins. 'Probably just a firework let off by someone trying to get festive,' said Raffety sarcastically as the 18:30 siren went off. 'Some chance.'

'Hey, wait for me!' he shouted, stumbling after his hungry dog into the unlit foyer of Tower Block 23.

Unknown to Raffety, the object that had almost taken his head off was something *from out of this world*.

THE PIXEL PAD

The weather these days was unpredictable and erratic electrical storms often caused power cuts across the country. To make things worse, the electricity to Tower Block 23 had been disconnected for years.

'All the more reason to eat raw carrots, Raffety,' Raffety's mum, Jenelope Ray, would reason. 'And counting steps is brilliant for improving your mental maths.'

It wasn't so brilliant for Raffety's head, shoulders, knees and shins, which all bore bruises from his regular falls.

'You need to *walk* up the stairs,' Raffety was always being told. But Raffety's clumsiness never dulled his enthusiasm for running.

Finally opening the front door, Raffety kicked off his boots while Wham shot through to the kitchen like a rocket. Dumping his school coat and jumper on the floor, Raffety followed.

'This one, this one, this one,' Wham panted, pawing madly at a tin of dog meat. 'Beef, beef, beef...' But Raffety was hungry, too. Taking a box of bangers and mash from the freezer, he ripped away the wrapping and threw it into the blaster. Setting the timer, he turned to the stack of tins by Wham's basket.

'What do you fancy Wham, boy?'

'Beef, beef, beef, beef, beef...' yapped Wham at a million yaps per second.

'I hear you,' said Raffety, picking up a can.

'No, no, no, no, no...' Wham whimpered when he saw the white, furry creature on the label.

'Rabbit!' cheered Raffety with gusto, forking out the entire tin. 'Your favourite.'

'No!!!' Wham collapsed onto his back, his paws stretched rigidly up to the ceiling. Just then,

Raffety heard his mum's mobile ringing.

'She must be getting a text alert about the ASBO,' he panicked.

Luckily, Mrs Ray was always so busy rushing between her jobs at Kick Start and the TiscoMart she was likely to leave her phone anywhere. Raffety found it by the toaster and, to his horror, an image of Dr Braincrammer, the headteacher at Barmy Towers School, flashed onto the screen accompanied by his automated voice:

'ASBO 6-3-2: R.S. Ray. 18:23.

Detention order issued.

Report to my office first thing

Boxing Day.'

'No!' Raffety exclaimed.

He deleted the text and chucked the phone in the bin. 'She'll buy another one,' he told himself.

Raffety then set off on his annual hunt for Christmas presents. As he suspected, his parent's wardrobe was stuffed full of them.

'Arrgh!' he cried in disgust when he saw all

the TLC logos. He rummaged through the lot, hoping to find a home-wrapped package.

'I knew it!' he groaned when he drew a blank.

Ignoring the retching sound coming from the kitchen, Raffety took the biggest parcel he could find and tore right into it.

'Rubbish!' he exclaimed when he saw the very same Pixel Pad they used in school. It was the very latest must-have TLC gizmo. 'Very educational,' people said.

'Very educational, my foot!' said Raffety now. He pulled out the pad and used the attached laser pen to draw a witch.

'Play,' he ordered when he was done.

Raffety's 2-D drawing jumped from the screen and instantly turned into 3-D hologram.

Three weeks ago Raffety had been part of the market research group that had given this Pixel Pad toy a big thumbs up at TLC HQ.

'You're the only child here that doesn't like it, boy,' the designer had scorned. 'What's your problem?'

'If I could draw droids and spaceships that transformed into 3-D models, I could see the point,' Raffety had gushed with excitement. 'I'd create my own interactive, intergalactic war game, become emperor of the universe and destroy every TLC factory on the planet.'

'No wonder your school test marks are so bad,' the designer had tutted.

Raffety's creative imagination led him to write countless fantastical stories.

'You can't spell and your grammar is awful,' his teacher was always telling him. 'Stop thinking so much and stick to the grammar exercises.'

Although Raffety got top marks in computing, his poor marks in grammar tests had resulted in him losing all Sunday play privileges. Instead, he had to attend these tedious market research sessions at TLC HQ.

'Choose a category,' the witch before him croaked.

'Hateful witches,' Raffety sneered.

'Category not recognized – try again,' squealed the witch.

Raffety was sure the voice belonged to Minister Geerta Crabwitch.

'Boring old farts,' Raffety goaded.

'Category not...'

'Evil ministers, ' Raffety went on. 'Wig wearers.' Crabwitch wore the wildest chrome-coloured wig Raffety had ever seen. 'Slime balls...'

'Six times twelve,' squawked the hologram, switching to a default quiz.

'Three,' said Raffety.

Whap! sounded the Pixel Pad horn.

'What is the capital of France?'

'Bognor.'

Whap!

'What two chemicals can be found in...?'

'Sulphur and Malodour,' Raffety interrupted, instantly recalling the formula for stink bombs.

Whap!

Mr Ray had reclaimed hundreds of old chemistry sets from the Heaps over the years. Raffety longed to detonate a stink bomb under one of his teachers but he was too scared.

'Any childish behaviour – any schoolboy pranks – and I promise the culprit will experience a reign of terror that will have them begging for a year of detentions,' Dr Braincrammer had bellowed in his first-day assembly.

Dr Braincrammer's office was famously crammed with hi-tech surveillance equipment that enabled him to see and hear everything that went on in the school. It also housed a chilling collection of electrical appliances designed to stimulate the brain. The scariest of all was an archaic, skull-shaped brainfrazzler, which Dr Braincrammer often took with him on random inspections, slamming it hard onto the scalp of anyone he felt like. The last boy who'd dared to commit a schoolboy prank had dribbled like a baby for hours after the brainfrazzler was used on him, and had been sent to Correction School for a whole year.

Raffety didn't hear his mum coming in through the front door.

'Why can't anyone hang a coat up around here?' she shouted from the hall. 'We've got the new neighbours popping round for coffee tomorrow. What will Mr and Mrs Chang think?'

'Mum will kill me if she finds this mess,' Raffety panicked, hastily stuffing the Pixel Pad and packaging back into the cupboard.

MEASURING UP
TO THE CHANGS

'Put your rubbish in the bin!!!' Mrs Ray yelled from the kitchen. 'We don't live on the streets – not yet. And where on Earth is my phone?'

Raffety knew he was in for it. He gingerly made his way down the hall.

'What's up with the dog?' Mrs Ray shouted. 'He's thrown up all over the floor.'

Raffety found his mum on her hands and knees, clearing up after Wham.

'He needs to see a vet,' sighed Mrs Ray, looking up.

Wham was rolling a tin of beef across the floor. Raffety recognized the eager look in the young mongrel's eyes and smiled.

'It's not a vet he needs, Mum,' said Raffety. 'It's a can opener.'

'Just open the bloomin' tin,' Wham barked.

'Wham's just trying to tell us he wants something else to eat,' Raffety told his mum.

'For goodness' sake, Raffety – he's a dog – he'll eat anything.'

'I'll eat you in a minute if you don't open this can,' Wham snarled.

'Watch it,' warned Mrs Ray, shaking a vomit-filled cloth towards Wham. 'There'll be no sofa privileges for you if you growl like that.'

Raffety opened the tin of beef and filled Wham's bowl.

'There ya go,' he said, giving Wham's furry head a good ruffle.

'Good boy,' Wham woofed, wagging his tail.

Mrs Ray got up and brushed herself down. 'Just look at my uniform,' she tutted. Mrs Ray was dressed in a dowdy brown suit issued by Kick Start, the government agency that got people back into the call centre and factory jobs once lost to the Chindia Federation.

'The Christmas pudding is on the table to defrost,' she told Raffety, sweeping back her long ginger hair. 'Just make sure you put in the fridge before you go to bed. The last thing we want is that dog eating it!'

Raffety examined the plastic mistletoe decorations and figured Wham wouldn't go anywhere near it. 'OK, Mum.'

'Right,' said Mrs Ray, tossing her dinner in the blaster. 'It's Christmas Eve. Let's put on the telly.'

Mrs Ray's cheery nature made her very popular at work. Unfortunately, her home life was rather testing but she usually managed to stay positive.

'I'm living with baboons!' she cried when she saw the mess in the living room.

Gathering up the clutter, Mrs Ray made her way to the computer. 'Mr Chang is a very important man at Kutan Studios,' she told Raffety. 'I don't want him thinking that people who work outside public broadcasting can't keep their homes in order.'

'Here we go,' thought Raffety. 'Now it's the Chang family we've all got to measure up to.'

'I thought all the important Kutan workers lived in Kutan World,' said Raffety.

'Clearly not,' replied Mrs Ray. 'Apparently their daughter is starting school with you on Boxing Day.'

'Really?'

'I told Mrs Chang that you'd be happy to walk her to school.'

'*Really*?'

Kutan Studios – in the capital city, Kutan – were at the epicentre of everything that happened in Raffety's world. Built over an area once called Milton Keynes, the enormous domed-shaped complex known as Kutan World housed not only the studios, but also the government and a luxury complex where all the eminent politicians and celebrities now lived.

While Raffety seethed at the prospect of walking the Chang's daughter to school, Mrs Ray typed the password for the home computer network. Suddenly, images of Geerta Crabwitch and Prime Minister Shrub burst onto the living room TV screen. Raffety squirmed with disgust.

'You will all have to work much harder next year...' Prime Minister Shrub was saying at the pre-Christmas news conference.

The Prime Minister was dressed in a gold sequined suit and tie, and his beard appeared speckled with pastry and sugar.

'They've been stuffing themselves with mince pies,' cried Raffety, spotting the big plate of them on the table.

'... You all wallowed and over-indulged yourselves during the economic boom years,' Minister Crabwitch gleefully interrupted, running her fingers through her insanely wild wig. 'You gorged yourselves on frivolous entertainment and now it's payback time. This government will not support slackers.'

'Sweet, coming from her,' Raffety interjected. 'She got a penthouse suite in Kutan World just because she was on that stupid super-nanny show.'

'She's only doing her job, Raffety,' called Mrs Ray from the kitchen as she took her piping-hot dinner from the blaster.

'And how does she get that electric-shock look in her wig and eyes?' Raffety wondered out loud.

'Raffety, you're being rude. Stop it right now,' his mum warned.

Despite their strict policies and rules, Prime Minister Shrub and Minister Crabwitch were surprisingly popular and still expected to win the next general election.

'They're crooks – both of them,' Mr Ray used to say.

These days he parroted the same line as everyone else: 'You have to admit, they've saved the economy.'

It drove Raffety mad. From what he could see, the trade deals made with the Chindia Federation – now the world's leading economic empire – meant his parents working for such low wages that they had to take on take on extra jobs just to survive. Mrs Ray came through carrying two trays.

'Looks like all the cosmetic surgery Minister Crabwitch has had recently really worked,' she said, cheerily. She handed Raffety his dinner and perched on the sofa to eat her own.

'Her skin's got more potholes than the moon,' Raffety squirmed in disbelief. 'They say she's had so much rat's pee pumped into her face she's starting to twitch like one.'

'Raffety Ray, wash your mouth out with soapy water at once!' cried Mrs Ray. 'That's a horrible thing to say!'

'Sorry, Mum,' Raffety mumbled.

'I don't want to hear you talking like that ever again.'

Now the image projected behind Crabwitch and the Prime Minister was of the Wall – the border that enclosed the old Greater London and urban sprawls as far north as Birmingham.

'It's an architectural wonder,' Mrs Ray sighed in awe.

'It is,' thought Raffety. 'I wonder *why* it's there at all.'

'Can I have some computer time in my room?' Raffety asked his mum. 'I need to visit the school website to get my Christmas Day homework.'

Like many kids living in President Shrub's New Britain, Raffety Ray had secretly worked out how to hack past the government-controlled intranet and onto the hyperweb. The problem was, President Shrub's new homeland security measures meant that these hyperweb visits had to be very brief because the cyberpolice were so fast in tracking down hackers.

After a few moments, Mrs Ray typed the release code for Raffety's personal computer.

'Thanks, Mum,' said Raffety, leaping up.

'And make sure you *walk* to your room,' said Mrs Ray. 'We've had complaints from the tenants downstairs.'

'Yes, Mum,' said Raffety as he bounded down the hall.

'And give your room a good tidy,' called Mrs Ray. 'There's so much rubbish on the floor I can't open the door.'

Raffety's bedroom was his sanctuary – a place where, in his mind, anything was possible.

And it was.

RAFFETY'S SECRET WORLD

With Wham panting at his heels, Raffety pushed his way into his bedroom and closed the door.

'It's great to be home,' he sighed, taking in the chaotic state of his toy workshop.

Raffety hoped one day to have his own toy company and a chain of shops crammed with amazing toys that he had invented. Kicking a pathway through all the rejected designs and prototypes for new toys strewn over the floor, Raffety switched on his computer and was soon channel-hopping from one celebrity show to the next. By chance, he clicked onto the TLC channel.

'When is anyone going to make a toy that

children can actually *play* with?' he groaned, disgusted with every single toy featured.

Raffety Ray had a dream. Zap Boy wasn't just an imaginary comic book superhero with a dog. He was on a one-boy mission to invent the ultimate toy – a toy that could change the world. From morning to night Raffety was obsessed – his mind a toyshop of ideas, so full of games, gadgets and fabulously interactive gizmos that there was little space left for all the facts Dr Braincrammer wanted to pack into his twelve-year-old brain. The only problem was, Raffety kept designing things that had already been invented, such as interlocking blocks – 'That's Lego,' his dad had happily reminisced, and shoes with wheels on – 'Roller-blades,' said his dad. These setbacks had pretty much knocked the wind right out of Raffety's sails. The truth, however, was that Raffety's recent designs were great. Like his latest – a hand-sized zapper. It was perfect for a superhero: streamlined, pocket-sized and, using a little imagination, had the power to zap the memory of anyone in range.

'A direct hit from this, and Mum and Dad will forget to check my test marks this week,' Raffety told Wham. 'And with just a few adjustments to the settings, I could finally get Dad to remember what actually happened to him the night of his arrest.'

If the zapper had actually been real, Raffety Ray might have taken his first small step towards becoming a real superhero. But as usual it was just an idea played out in his very vivid imagination.

'Let's check the blog,' said Raffety, hacking onto the hyperweb to get to his blog.

'Let's chill out,' thought Wham, curling up on the bed.

It had been nearly a month since Raffety had begun his Zap Boy blog. Protected by his hidden, superhero identity, Raffety was fond of raising dangerous questions to blog about. Questions such as: 'Why can't we play?' 'Why are there no storybooks anywhere?' 'What really happens at Correction School?' And his favourite, 'Who's ready to fight back?'

'No messages *again*,' Raffety sighed when the page came up. Feeling dejected, Raffety quickly clicked back to the TV.

'Kids are too scared to even log on, let alone write something,' he told Wham.

But Wham had other things on his mind or, rather, on his bladder. 'I should have gone for a pee,' he was thinking.

Raffety ripped off his school tie and yanked his shirt over his head. Changing into jeans and his precious Zap Boy T-Shirt (the one with ZAP! plastered in big letters across the front), Raffety spent a few minutes scribbling down some ideas for his next *Zap Boy* comic.

'I'm off to TiscoMart,' Mrs Ray called down the hall. 'I'm on the checkout until one. Remember to put the Christmas pudding in the fridge. Bye.'

'See you,' Raffety responded absent-mindedly, lost in the world of Zap Boy.

An hour or so later the grind of a dumper truck outside caught Raffety's attention. Laying down his pencil, he stepped over to the window and looked out.

'I need a pee,' Wham barked.

Among the bin men in grey overalls wheeling bins from all corners of the estate, was the tall, lanky figure of Raffety's dad. Mr Ray saw his son at the window and waved.

'Better get to bed, son,' he hollered loudly, so Raffety could hear him over the engine. 'You know the TLC pixies won't come until you're fast asleep.'

Raffety squirmed, embarrassed that the neighbours might have overheard. 'I'm eleven,' he muttered. 'Why's Dad such a jerk these days?'

'I need a pee,' Wham barked a little louder.

Raffety watched the bin men at work while the TV aired an advert for the Pixel Pad.

'Children should not be seen or heard!' Minister Crabwitch screeched.

'What a great idea,' thought Raffety Ray, imagining a toy which could make children both invisible and inaudible to adults.

'I-Need-A-Pee!' Wham barked, as if talking to an idiot.

'Relax,' said Raffety calmly, stroking

Wham's head. 'I'll get you a drink in a minute.'

Wham banged his head against the window; breathing out with such a long, beefy sigh of frustration that he steamed up the whole thing. Raffety rubbed his sleeve over the glass. He was about to turn away when he saw footprints appearing in the snow. Nothing unusual about that, only Raffety couldn't see *anyone* out there.

ROUGH
PENCILS

THE SPY
NEXT DOOR

Raffety was pondering on the weirdness of the bodiless footprints when he saw the white, hazy outline of what appeared to be a small animal in trouble.

'It's freaking out,' he exclaimed, jumping from the bed, 'Come on, Wham!'

'At last!' Wham barked, leaping from the windowsill.

Raffety grabbed a torch and within seconds boy and dog were pelting down the hall.

Bursting out into the bitterly cold night, Raffety ran to the bins and shone his torch all around.

'Calm down, boy,' he hushed his dog. 'There's a scared animal out here. I don't want you...' Suddenly Raffety realized that Wham was nowhere to be seen. 'Wham?'

CU-TUSH!

'That feels so much better,' Wham howled happily from behind the bins. He was just shaking his back leg when a new trail of footprints suddenly appeared in the snow nearby.

Raffety followed the footprints with his torch.

'Don't be scared,' he hushed through chattering teeth.

Wham buried his head between Raffety's legs.

'Not you,' Raffety snapped.

For a moment, Wham's tail and ears drooped visibly.

'What is that?!' Raffety exclaimed, as small droplets of snow formed a thin, ghostly outline before them.

'Rabbit?' Wham shivered, feeling his stomach recoil.

Raffety crouched down for a closer look.

'It's like an inside-out snow globe,' he gasped in awe, remembering a Christmas decoration he hadn't seen for years.

Raffety heard the whir of a camera.

'ASBO,' blurted the computer. 'This camera is recording your...'

'Oh, go away!' Raffety shouted; he was in so much trouble now he didn't care. 'Dr Braincrammer can rant and rave all he likes,' he thought. 'He can't stop this.' He shuffled a little closer, blocking the camera's view of whatever it was that was forming before their eyes.

'Don't be scared,' he whispered. 'We won't hurt you.'

There was a scattering of snow in mid-air and then a scurrying sound as more footprints appeared in the snow.

'It's coming to get me,' Wham whimpered, pressing his head against Raffety's thigh.

Raffety held out the palm of his right hand.

'Come on,' he whispered. 'Don't be afraid.'

The footprints moved closer. 'It's standing right in front of me!' Raffety shivered with

excitement. He put down his torch and laid out both his palms.

'Hop on and I'll take you inside,' he said, quietly.

He reached out with one hand, felt something warm and furry, and started to stroke it.

'I'm going to pick you up,' he said softly as he gently lifted the trembling creature onto his other hand.

Nestling the scarcely visible animal into his arms, Raffety picked up his torch and headed back to the flats.

'I'm going to take you somewhere safe and warm,' he whispered.

'This just cannot be happening,' Wham whimpered as he followed at a safe distance.

As they reached the third-floor corridor, Raffety stared at the sight of a figure standing in the dark outside his front door.

'Who are you?' he gasped, stopping dead in his tracks. The creature in his arms was virtually invisible but Raffety still turned his body to shield it from the figure.

Raising his torch, Raffety saw that it was a girl in Chindi trainers, jeans and T-shirt.

'You goofball,' he chastised himself when he realized that he hadn't shut the door to the flat.

'My name's Sky,' said the girl.

'Spy?' Raffety blurted.

The girl was pretty, with dark skin, dark hair and almond-shaped eyes. Raffety was wary of her. 'What if she has sneaked in and had a poke around my room?' he panicked.

'*Sky*,' said the girl, crossly.

Raffety screwed up his face.

'Why would anyone name a girl after the sky?' he wondered.

'*Sky*, as in the cable TV network they had back in the olden days,' she explained, irritated by Raffety's expression.

'Oh,' said Raffety, dumbly.

'I was just standing here to make sure no burglars got in. I saw your mum go off to the TiscoMart.'

'How do you know where my mum works?' Raffety challenged as he edged towards the door.

'You lot shout,' said Sky flatly. 'And these walls are as thin as tin.'

'Thanks,' said Raffety, sarcastically. 'You're very neighbourly. Must go.'

He chased Wham into the flat and slammed the door.

'Her dad works at Kutan Studios,' thought Raffety, nervously, his back against the door. 'What if Sky is some sort of government spy?'

WONDER

Once he had got his breath back, Raffety went straight to the kitchen. Keeping the creature nestled in the crook of his arm, he began rooting through the cupboards. With packets, boxes and tins cascading and spilling all around him, he eventually dug out a box of icing sugar.

'Where did Mum put that old sieve?' he pondered, beginning another messy rummage.

When he had everything he needed, Raffety went to his room.

'Now, I need you to sit still,' Raffety told his mystery guest. He swept his arm across the tabletop to clear a space and carefully put the invisible creature down. 'This is icing sugar.

It won't hurt.'

Wham jumped onto the bed for a better view.

'He can't want another pet *surely*,' he grumbled. 'He can hardly cope with me.'

As the last droplets of black slush dripped from the creature's body, Raffety held the sieve right over the spot where he imagined its head to be and tipped up the box of icing sugar. The entire contents fell into the sieve like a brick, sending a cloud of fine sugar up into the air.

'A-choo!' Raffety sneezed.

The puff of sugar reminded Raffety of the magic tricks his dad used to perform for him when he was a kid. This illusion, however, was so wonderfully real that Raffety almost squealed with joy. The icing sugar was crystallizing against the creature's warm, wet body, sticking like candyfloss to every part of it and revealing the outline of a furry-looking creature with pointy ears and a big bushy tail.

'He looks so cute,' thought Raffety.

'What an ugly thing,' Wham grumbled.

The creature had covered his eyes with monkey-like paws.

'What are you?' Raffety stammered.

As far as Raffety could tell, the sugar-coated creature – who was about thirty centimetres tall – was a cross between a bush baby and a cuddly chinchilla. 'He's terrified, the poor thing,' thought Raffety, realizing that the creature was shaking all over. 'Maybe he's scared of the light.'

He dimmed the lights. Then, rifling through the mess on the floor, he picked out the toy sunglasses that had once belonged his Action Man – confiscated like so many other of his toys after the police raid. Raffety gently moved the creature's paws away and slipped the shades over his eyes. Then, slowly lowering his paws to his sides, the creature looked timidly up into Raffety's awestruck eyes and, to his amazement, started to sing!

'*Ah-he-hoo, hoo-he-ah, ah-he-hoo, hoo-he-ah...*'

In a sweet, gentle voice – almost human in

its tone – the creature held a tune so beautiful and sad it sent a tingle down Raffety's spine.

'You're trying to tell me that you feel sad,' said Raffety, feeling an empathetic tear form in his eye.

'*Ah-he-hoo, hoo-he-ah, ah-he-hoo, hoo-he-ah,*' the creature repeated, only this time, the sound was accompanied by a sequence of soft, luminous colours – first orange, then lemon, then red, blue and indigo, before switching to a never-ending strobe of colourful patterns that illuminated his whole body.

'Wow!' Raffety cried as he took in the visual splendour. 'You're an alien – you've got to be.'

Then something really amazing happened. From a 'kangaroo pouch' low down on its stomach, the creature took out a small, round interface.

'What's that?' asked Raffety, moving closer to get a better look at the monitor and controls. The creature quickly pressed a sequence of tiny buttons, and suddenly the whole bedroom was filled with images of a spectacular 3-D galaxy of floating planets and stars.

As the creature continued to sing, a wide spaceship, several decks high and flanked by hundreds of star-fighters, appeared to float across the bedroom.

'Wow! You really *are* an alien from another world,' Raffety gasped. Raffety Ray had a vivid imagination, but never in his life had he dreamed up anything like this.

'You're trying to tell me that this is your spaceship,' said Raffety, realizing that the excited alien was repeatedly pointing to the lead star-fighter in the fleet.

'You're a star-fighter pilot,' .
exclaimed. 'And a really important one at tha.

But Raffety wasn't the only Earthly creature inspired by the alien's visual display and his haunting lament. Somewhere in Dog World, Wham was really getting into the groove, '*Ah-he-hoo, hoo-he-ah, ah-he-hoo, hoo-he-ah...*' he echoed, feeling an uncontrollable urge to join in. Unfortunately, Wham's tune got a little lost in translation.

'Oh, Wham, *please* shut up,' Raffety begged as Wham howled like a transforming werewolf. But Wham was spellbound and no amount of persuasion could get him to stop.

'You really are a wonder!' Raffety sighed happily when the alien finally stopped singing and the display faded away. He paused while his words floated around in his head. And then he had an idea. 'That's what I'll call you,' Raffety smiled. 'Wonder.'

'Won-door,' the alien mimicked. 'Won-door.'

Deep in thought, Raffety made his way over to the window and stared into the darkness. 'How did he get here?' he thought.

He recalled the dazzling streak of light that had flashed before his eyes just before curfew. 'I thought it was a firework,' he mumbled, looking down at the bins. 'But it must have been a small spaceship.'

Raffety felt a soft, warm prod on his arm. He looked down to see Wonder standing on the sill beside him and pointing urgently down to the bins.

'*Aki-ko-fi-tu,*' said Wonder, his voice much higher and staccato now.

Then Raffety had a horrible thought.

'Wonder!' he exclaimed. 'They emptied the bins an hour ago.'

Wonder looked confused.

'Your spaceship,' cried Raffety. 'It's gone to the Heaps!'

THINK 'HUSKY'

Raffety ran to his parents' bedroom and began rummaging through all the drawers.

'There's a key in here somewhere, I know it,' he said out loud.

'No-it, no-it...' echoed Wonder, eager to practise Earth talk.

'Woof,' went Wham.

'Woof, woof...' Wonder aped, which sent Wham into an excitable yowling rant.

Raffety yanked out his dad's bedside drawer and tipped its contents out on the bed.

'Mum's right!' he gasped, mystified by the random array of junk. 'Dad really is a kleptomaniac.'

'Main-ee-ak, main-ee-ak...' Wonder copied.

'Please stop!' Raffety exclaimed, slamming his hands over his ears. 'You're not a parrot.'

'Pa-rrot, pa-rrot...' Wonder chanted with his paws over his ears.

'What if Wonder isn't a top star-fighter at all?' Raffety panicked. 'What if he's like Jake Harrison? Rubbish at everything and never shuts up.'

But there was no time to dwell on this. Raffety's dad still rented the garage in which he'd once stored the greatest collection of antique toys from the late 1990s that Raffety had ever seen.

'We need transport,' said Raffety. 'If we don't get to the Heaps fast, Wonder's spaceship will be lost forever.'

'Space-ship, space-ship...' Wonder repeated, practising this strange new language.

Then, a stroke of luck.

'Let's go!' Raffety shouted, grabbing the big bunch of keys he had just found.

Within minutes, Raffety was wrapped up in

his grey school overcoat and gloves and standing with Wham and Wonder outside his dad's garage. Against a cacophony of barks, grunts and countless automated ASBOs, Raffety tried key after key after key.

'None of them works!' he finally cried, giving the door a big kick with his boot. A bolt of lightning shot past his ear.

'*Hi-ya!*' Wonder squealed as the lock exploded.

'Ow!' Raffety exclaimed, feeling a sizzling heat in his ear. 'You could have blown my head off!'

Wonder jumped to the ground. 'Spaceship,' he shouted, his fur flashing red.

'Cool it with the lights,' Raffety hushed as he pulled up the metal door. 'You're creating a scene. Boys my age should be in bed. It's the law.'

But in a dark garage, Wonder's light was exactly what they needed. Raffety picked up a harness attached to an old sledge.

'Wham!' he cheered, shooting Wham a motivating look. 'Think "Husky".'

'Urgh?'

A scruffy, ginger-haired boy charging down the road on a sledge is quite a sight. Add to that, a wild-looking mongrel where the husky should be and a lightshow from an alien in shades and you've got a surefire head-turner. But when the only heads around belong to fellow law-breakers, and the driving black sleet is blurring every surveillance camera around, anything goes.

Raffety got Wham to take the short cut through Notting Hill.

'They don't get streetscum around here,' he told Wonder as they zoomed past the high walls and electronic gates of the houses.

'They're scared of the ...'

'Pit bulls!' yelped Wham, yanking on the harness as he pulled for his life.

Raffety glanced back at the pack of ferocious canines charging out of an opening gate.

'Faster!' Wham yapped, thinking Raffety was pushing.

'Faster!' shouted Raffety, swishing the reins.

'*Hi-ya!*' Wonder exclaimed, firing multicoloured lasers from his interface.

Wonder's lasers were igniting like firecrackers around the pit bulls' heads.

'That's one cool zapper, Wonder,' Raffety cheered, seeing the dogs freak out. He stared with envy at the strange round handset in Wonder's paws. 'Just how many settings has that thing got?' he thought.

With the sleet pummelling into their faces, they sledged on towards the black clouds looming over the Kensington Heaps.

'We'll find your spaceship,' Raffety told Wonder. 'I promise.'

But, in truth, Raffety was scared.

'The Heaps are extremely dangerous,' his parents had warned him a thousand times. 'You must never go there.'

As they drew nearer to the Heaps, the roar of the wind turbines almost masked the sound of an approaching storm.

'Yuk!' spat Raffety as a vile black vapour

grabbed the back of his throat. He buried his face under his coat.

Wham, clearly exhausted, was starting to slow down.

'Hang on, Wonder,' called Raffety, wrapping a hand around the alien on his shoulder. He jumped off the sledge and placed Wonder gently down in the slush.

'I'm dead,' Wham whimpered, collapsing in a heap, steam pluming up from his coat.

A bolt of lightning ripped through the sky.

'I can't believe people actually live here,' Raffety squirmed at the sight of the ice-holes and hovels on the outskirts of the Heaps. 'They call the people who live here "streetscum",' he told Wonder. 'The government blame them for everything.'

There was a loud blast. Raffety and Wonder threw themselves down into the slush as a huge flame jettisoned up into the sky.

'Aerosol cans,' said Raffety, recalling his dad's tales from the Heaps. He pulled himself up and looked out at the small clans of people huddled around fires all over the Heaps.

'Pretty soon someone's going to see me and ask why I'm here,' he trembled, realizing how out of place looked in his smart school overcoat and boots. 'And they'll lynch me!'

He ripped off his coat and tossed it away. Fumbling through a pile of soaking-wet rubbish nearby, he picked out a raincoat, punctured and torn beyond repair, and put it on. He was just scuffing up his boots on a concrete slab when...

'Hey! That's my coat.'

Raffety leapt back in terror.

SCAVENGING

Raffety looked around, trying to find the person who had shouted at him with such anger. But there was no one.

'What if I'm attacked?' he shuddered. The raincoat felt cold and horribly clingy – a real problem if he had to run.

'Better get your zapper ready,' Raffety whispered to Wonder, shivering at his feet.

Then, through a chink in a corrugated metal door they saw something move.

'I've got a dog,' Raffety shouted. 'He's vicious, so watch out.'

Wham was still crashed out in the harness, dreaming of snacks in a woolly-lined basket.

Raffety peered closer and saw that many pairs of eyes were peering out at them. Raffety scooped up Wonder into his arms.

'Wham, wake up,' he whispered as he untied the harness. Then, realizing that Wham was still half asleep: 'Biscuits.'

Wham's ears shot up. Raffety grabbed one.

'Ow!' Wham yelped, as he was yanked away.

They hid behind a burnt-out car wreck and surveyed the scrubscape through the fiery haze.

'There must be a hundred dumper trucks and diggers working in here,' Raffety thought. Another bolt of lightning tore through the sky followed by a deafening roll of thunder. Wonder huddled up tight in Raffety's arms. '*Ata-ka,*' he shivered.

They watched the diggers for a while as the machines shovelled huge piles of rubbish into massive, smog-belching incinerators. Wham started to yap.

'What is it, boy?'

Raffety followed Wham's gaze.

'You're right, boy,' he cheered, ruffling
Wham's head. 'It's Dad.'

Mr Ray was directing a dumper truck as it
reversed towards one of the Heaps. 'Right,
Wonder, this is it,' Raffety said as he lowered him
down again. 'Your spaceship is about to be
dumped on that heap over there. Better keep
make yourself invisible and stay close.'

Right now, Wonder's ability to become invisible at will was something Raffety envied.

The truck and crew were just leaving for their final round of the night when the heavens opened. 'We need to move *now*!' cried Raffety as scavengers swarmed in for anything they could eat, use or sell.

It was as if the doors had opened on a sale. Remembering the star-fighters that Wonder had shown them, Raffety and Wham were soon clambering with the scavengers across all the rotting food, clothes, packaging, bulbs, monitors, phones — every useless, discarded, damaged thing imaginable — as they hunted for his spaceship.

Pausing for breath, Raffety became shockingly aware of how many children there were around him. 'And nearly all of them are younger than me!' he thought. But Raffety was soon back on his task, so focused now on finding Wonder's spaceship that his eyes barely left the ground. But the pummelling rain was making conditions increasingly treacherous.

'Better get away!' someone shouted. 'The diggers are coming!'

He felt a tug on his arm and looked up to see a girl in a grey coat, her eyes burning with terror.

'What?' Raffety stammered.

'Come with me now or you'll be sucked into an incinerator and burnt to a crisp!'

She grabbed Raffety's hand as the rubbish began to slide away beneath his feet. Terrified, Raffety felt himself plunging into the darkness, his arms and legs kicking uselessly around him, while all the time feeling the girl's painfully tight grip on his hand. Unable to breathe, he was about to pass out when she gave a final, violent tug – and he felt firm ground beneath his feet.

'Wham!' he gasped, craning his head around. 'Wonder!'

He yanked himself free and looked around anxiously.

'You can't go back,' wheezed the girl, her face flushed with exhaustion. 'You'll be killed!'

Raffety shielded his eyes from the rain and scanned the Heaps, 'Where are they? Where are they...?' he cried repeatedly.

Then there was an awful, spine-chilling howl.

REBEL HIDEOUT

Raffety saw Wham burrowing like mad into the rubbish. 'He's trying to save Wonder,' he gasped.

He watched in horror as a digger scooped Wham up with the rubbish.

'No!!!' Raffety screamed, stumbling after the digger.

He saw Wham's petrified face peep over the shovel as it swung through the air.

'Jump, Wham. Jump for your life!' Raffety shouted.

He ran toward the digger but was pushed to the ground by a man in a green, hypothermal jumpsuit.

'Shove off, streetscum,' the man growled,

raising a baseball bat.

Raffety scrambled past him and up the mountain of rubbish just as Wham leapt from the shovel. Opening his arms, Raffety broke Wham's fall and together they tumbled over and over. When they finally came to a stop they were both dizzy and disorientated.

'Where's Wonder?' Raffety begged as Wham shook himself out.

You didn't need to understand Dog Talk to understand the depressing pain in Wham's howl. Raffety hugged Wham hard.

'It's not your fault,' he sobbed.

'TAGGERS!' yelled the girl, catching up with Raffety and grabbing his hand again. Another flash of lightning tore up the sky. Raffety looked up to see three burly men in green, all armed with baseball bats, heading straight for them.

They ran, splashing through the fast-flowing river of debris, the men in pursuit. But the girl knew the Heaps better than anyone. Zigzagging through the flooded alleyways she finally led Raffety and Wham to the outskirts of the dump.

'That's my sledge,' Raffety panted when he saw it drifting away in the filth. He ran over and dragged it back. With the pressure of the taggers gone, Raffety finally noticed what the girl was wearing.

'That's my coat,' he spluttered.

'And that's mine,' said the girl, pointing to Raffety's shabby old raincoat.

Soaked to the skin and with Wham whining at his side, Raffety had a strange thought.

'Do I know you?' he asked, cautiously.

The girl's long blonde hair was clamped like cling film around her soaked head.

'You did once,' she said, glumly. 'My name's Anna Polanski. I was at the same school as you for a while.' Raffety trawled his memory. 'Anna Polanski...' he pondered. 'Then... weren't your family on that Crabwitch *Super Nanny* programme on Channel 52?' he asked. 'You were the one naughty kid that Crabwitch couldn't squash. We loved you. You always got the better of her – it was brilliant.'

'Was it?' mumbled the girl.

'Your parents got into big trouble because they wrote and published children's books – even after they were banned,' he said, a little calmer. 'They got sentenced to seven years' hard labour on the Wall.'

He looked at the tears spilling from Anna's brown eyes and felt really awful that he had spoken so tactlessly.

'I'm sorry,' he murmured.

Anna looked a bit wobbly. Raffety offered his hand, but she didn't take it.

'The year Crabwitch became Minister of Child Development she hunted me down,' said Anna. 'I had three years of Corrective School before I got away.'

'You escaped?' exclaimed Raffety in disbelief.

'Not just me,' said Anna. 'Follow me.'

She led Raffety to a well-hidden hovel and pulled back a sheet of corrugated iron.

'Our hideout,' she said, gesturing inside. 'The whole school came with me.'

Raffety peered into the gloom where as many as fifty children in rags, some only five years old, were huddled up around an assortment of lights wired up to old car batteries.

'It's all right,' Anna called, quietly. 'His name is Raffety Ray. I used to be at his school.'

*   *   *

That night, around a plastic Christmas tree illuminated with twinkly silver lights, the children were all eager to talk.

'It's my fault that he died,' said Raffety miserably when he told the children about

69

Wonder. 'I should have been looking after him.'

Raffety was comforted with many words of condolence from the children, who clearly all thought that Wonder was his pet.

The children showed Raffety how they prepared food and hot drinks on rusty cookers wired up to old car batteries.

'We usually find some food that we can just about eat,' Anna explained. 'But we're always hungry.'

Raffety was keen to learn more about Correction School.

'They force you to watch video lectures of Minister Crabwitch for hours and hours and hours,' said one boy. 'And then they test you on what she said.'

'And if you get things wrong they stick you in a dark room and a computer fires random facts at you until you can hardly hear yourself think,' interjected a girl, handing Raffety a mug of hot broth.

Raffety heard too how the children used old computers from the dump to surf the hyperweb and chat with other street kids all over the country.

'The Cyber Police never bother us,' Anna told him. 'And in some ways we have more freedom now than ever before – but it comes at a price.'

Many children showed Raffety scars around their wrists and ankles.

'It's the taggers from the mines,' Anna shuddered. 'If they catch you they clap on tracking irons that send out electric shocks whenever they need you.'

'Need you for what?' asked Raffety, feeling shocked and stupid.

'For mining,' quivered a small girl, scratching her matted brown hair. 'Don't you know anything?'

'The coal mines beyond the Wall,' Anna told Raffety. 'The government are desperate for electricity and they'll do anything to get it.'

'And when the kids become too tired to work in the mines any more, they're just abandoned,' said a boy, around Raffety's age, his chin marked with a scar. 'Left with nothing to defend themselves with against the wild rabid dogs and wolves.'

Raffety was overwhelmed. 'And to think I was cross about getting only TLC toys for Christmas,' he thought, hanging his head in shame.

'Hey,' said Anna, giving Raffety a shake. 'The storm's passing.'

Raffety checked his watch.

'It's nearly midnight,' he mumbled, getting up. 'I have to go.'

'I don't suppose we'll ever see you again,' said Anna.

'I'll come back tomorrow,' said Raffety, trying to muster a smile. 'I promise.' He'd already decided to come back with as much food as he could carry.

Anna offered Raffety his coat and torch, but Raffety wouldn't take them.

'Don't get caught on camera,' she warned him, putting an old blanket over his head. 'The authorities have far worse punishments than

Correction School to deal with rebels – you know that now.' She pulled back the corrugated metal 'door'.

Raffety and Wham dragged the sledge back through the slush. It was 00:57 by the time they got back to Tower Block 23.

'We've just beaten Mum's taxi,' said Raffety, seeing a cruiser turn into the road.

He dumped the old blanket and raincoat in the foyer and then felt his way up the stairs and down the corridor in complete darkness. As he fumbled his key into the lock, Raffety looked down at his bedraggled dog,

'Looks like we made it, Wham boy,' he sighed, unaware of the dim chink of light coming through the letterbox of the flat across the hallway.

CYBERSPACE
AND BEYOND

That night, Raffety had nightmares. With Wham at his heels and Wonder clasped in his arms, he was surrounded by raging fires and splashing through a junk-filled river – desperate to escape an army of axe-wielding giants led by an enraged Geerta Crabwitch.

'I'm on to you now, Raffety Ray,' Crabwitch bellowed, cracking her whip at the vicious black dogs that pulled her dark chariot.

Raffety sat bolt upright in bed, sweat pouring down his face.

'Wonder!' he cried.

The misery of losing his alien friend was

something Raffety had hardly begun to process.

Ignoring his Christmas stocking, Raffety went to the kitchen to find – a bombsite of mauled-open boxes, Christmas presents, dog biscuits and...

'The Christmas pud!' he cried, staring at the empty plate on the table. 'I forgot to put it in the fridge.' His eyes shot to Wham's basket. 'Wham!'

But Wham was in Dog Heaven, stomach full, fast asleep and with his new squeaking bone tucked safely under his pillow.

'Mum's going to go ballistic,' Raffety groaned through gritted teeth.

Taking a bacon butty from the freezer, Raffety threw it in the blaster and quickly set the timer. As he did, he thought of the children he had met last night at the Heaps. 'I have so much compared with them,' he thought as he made a pathetic attempt to shove things into cupboards. 'It's not right that children live on the streets and slave in government mines,' he said out loud, feeling his anger bubbling up. 'It's not right that even lucky kids like me who have a home still have to cram their heads with useless facts, ten hours a day, six days a week!' His mind was sizzling now with rage. 'Zap Boy wouldn't stand for this. He'd fight back. Start a revolution. He'd...'

BANG!

'You goofball!' Raffety chastised himself, as smoke rose from the blaster. 'You left the packaging on the butty.'

The fire alarm kicked in. Raffety lurched for the red 'off' button but was blinded by spray from the sprinklers.

'Where am I?' Wham spluttered.

Finally, after an embarrassing kerfuffle with tea towels, oven gloves and a grumpy wet dog, Raffety managed to restore some order.

'What's going on?!' Mr Ray shouted down the corridor. 'It's the middle of the night.'

It was gone ten in the morning but Raffety didn't quibble.

'It's all right, Dad,' he called. 'I've got it all under control.'

'Open your presents and watch the telly,' Mr Ray grumbled. 'Just wake me up for the speech at three.'

'Yes, Dad.'

Geerta Crabwitch made a speech at 15:00 every Christmas Day. Everyone watched it. They had to because there were random tests on it at school and at work to catch the slackers.

'I don't feel good,' Wham whimpered, curling up in his basket.

Chucking the remains of his butty into the bin, Raffety returned to his room.

'I'll make something useful for Anna Polanski,' he thought. 'That's what Zap Boy would do.'

But seeing the icing sugar and sieve on his table only reminded him of Wonder.

'This is the worst Christmas ever!' Raffety wailed, throwing himself on the bed.

Raffety had no idea how long he lay there thumping the pillow. He didn't hear the quiet tapping sound at the window. He didn't hear his dog howl or, as predicted, his mum going ballistic in the kitchen. What he did hear was a weird, mournful melody.

Raffety jumped out of bed and threw back the curtains.

'Wonder!' he cheered, seeing the forlorn-looking alien perched precariously on the sill. Raffety's heart was racing with excitement. He tried to force open the window.

'It's a bit stiff since Dad painted it,' Raffety grimaced as he pushed. 'Move along a bit.' He gestured with his head while he continued to bang the frame. 'If the window flies open it will knock you ri –'

The window flew open and Wonder plummeted from the sill.

'No!!!' Raffety cried, following his fall.

He waited for the SPLAT of alien hitting concrete, but just metres from the ground Wonder simply spread his arms and glided effortlessly upwards. Within seconds he was back on the sill.

'Wonder fly,' he said with a grin.

'You fly *and* talk!!!' Raffety exclaimed.

Wonder was soaking wet and smelled fairly grim, so Raffety ran to the bathroom for a damp flannel and towel.

'Hey, slow down,' said Raffety, dodging the sparks as Wonder rubbed himself down. By the time he was through, Wonder had seriously static fur.

'I thought you were dead,' Raffety told Wonder. 'I felt awful. Like it was all my fault.'

Wonder was too busy trying to brush down his fur to follow Raffety's guilty admission.

'And I'm so sorry about your spaceship,' Raffety went on.

Wonder reached into his pouch and pulled out a clump of wires and shiny silver balls.

'Is that all that's left of it?' asked Raffety, aghast.

Wonder looked really miserable and, to his shame, Raffety was aware of a feeling that somehow this was a good thing. 'He'll have to stay here on Earth,' he thought, contemplating how good it could be to have a powerful alien friend so close at hand. 'I'll help you build a new one,' he told Wonder, feeling guilty and without the slightest idea how.

He tried to think what he could do to cheer up Wonder.

'You must be hungry,' he said.

'Hun-gry?' Wonder repeated, looking puzzled.

Raffety used mime to explain 'hungry'.

'Hungry,' Wonder agreed, copying the actions.

Raffety ran down to the kitchen to blast some food.

'So there you are!' exclaimed his mum when Raffety burst into the kitchen. Dressed in pyjamas, dressing gown and pink poodle slippers,

Mrs Ray was armed with a mop and was clearly ready to use it.

'You could have killed him!' she shouted.

Raffety was suddenly struck by an awful stench.

'Christmas pudding is much too rich for a dog,' Mrs Ray went on.

'You're telling me,' said Wham with a belch from his basket. 'And those spiky green leaves really tear at your throat.'

'Look, Mum –' Raffety started.

But Mrs Ray wasn't listening.

'We've got the Chang family coming round for morning coffee, and Grandpa Ray, Aunt May and *who knows* how many of your father's banking buddies joining us for dinner. You are NOT leaving this kitchen until you've cleaned up after that smelly dog – who, by the way, is going straight to the kennels the next time he farts in here!'

Raffety glanced at Wham's hangdog eyes peeping up from his basket.

'I was hungry,' Wham whimpered.

Raffety helped his mum tidy up and quickly blasted some apple pie for Wonder.

'And I want you eating a proper breakfast,' his mum nagged, tossing Raffety a packet of fruit bars.

With a disgraced Wham lumbering at his side, Raffety returned to his room. They found Wonder on the table, his arms moving at an incredible speed as he pieced together one of Raffety's old model star-fighters. As soon as Wham saw Wonder, he started to barked excitedly and leapt up to greet him.

'Wham's happy to see you,' Raffety smiled, as Wham licked Wonder all over. 'He was as upset as I was when we lost you.'

Admiring Wonder's work, Raffety idly put down the fruit bars and apple pie. Wonder ate them avidly but his hunger to explore Raffety's designs and prototypes soon had him examining the zappers, the racing cars, the planes and, of course, the spaceships to be found around his room. And while he delved, Wonder sang, accompanied by Wham's horrible drone.

'Look, keep it down,' Raffety hushed, thinking of Sky Chang. 'The walls are as thin as tin.'

To quieten things down, Raffety switched on his computer and hacked onto the hyperweb. He was about to check his blog when Wonder briskly pushed him aside and started surfing.

'*Uba-uba-uba*...' Wonder chanted, with great enthusiasm while he typed furiously at the keys.

Raffety figured that Wonder must have found some cyber-portal in the hyperweb because suddenly he burst through into a fantastical world, sparkling in bright, iridescent colours, that seemed to fill not only the screen but the whole bedroom.

'WOW!!!' cried Raffety, totally transfixed by the apparent simulation around them.

But this cyberworld was more real than Raffety could ever imagine, connecting him to powers beyond all human understanding. Powers that would change his life forever.

THE BEST
CHRISTMAS
PRESENT – EVER!

'Is that your home?' gasped Raffety as he gaped at his monitor, 'It's beautiful!' It felt as if they were flying through a lush, multi-coloured landscape scattered with extraterrestrials.

Like all dogs, Wham understood all languages – even alien as it turned out – and as Wonder jabbered away in his mother tongue, Wham found that he understood pretty much everything.

'Stop Empress Ogoron diverting Earth's power,' Wham translated to himself. 'Uaan-4 in great danger.'

Suddenly, it looked to Raffety as if they were zooming towards a magnificent chrome palace. The entrance swept open to reveal a spectacular hall filled with creatures and objects that Raffety couldn't begin to comprehend.

'What's happening?' he asked nervously when the picture started to fragment.

It soon became clear that the cyber connection was getting weaker. Then the screen went blank. Raffety turned to Wonder.

'Wonder, I need you. There are so many things I want to do but I can't – not on my own.'

Wonder understood the words but was puzzled by what the Raffety thought he could do for him. 'The Earthling has so few powers,' he thought. 'And I have my own mission.'

He could never have guessed that his own mission and the ambitions of his new friend would have so much in common. Pinned to the back of the bedroom door was a wish list for his ultimate toy. Raffety got it down.

'What I need is a toy that can help me fly and make me invisible,' he started, using the list as a prompt. 'It also needs to convert into a star-fighter,' he went on excitedly, 'take me through space and time, download any cartoon and comic in the world, oh, and do *all* my homework.'

'If it can get me into a tin of beef, I'm in,' Wham muttered.

Wonder looked totally bamboozled.

'Of course, it doesn't have to do *all* that stuff,' said Raffety, feeling a bit greedy. 'But if it can be nifty and easy to hide, that would be good too.'

Realizing that Wonder was still confused, Raffety set about miming his way through the list: zooming round the room with his arms stretched out wide, jumping off the bed – anything that came into his head.

'The Earthling wants everything,' he thought sadly. 'Earthling has much to learn.'

Wonder knew from his research that Earth's technology was very primitive. Unless he was going to try the old Uaan initiation ceremony on the boy – a power transference that had never been tested on other races – his only hope of achieving what he thought the Earthling wanted was to create a link with the master computer on Uaan-4. But did the boy have something they could use? Deciding on this as the best course of action, Wonder leapt up onto the shelves, tipped out a box full of old mobile phones and took the best one he could find.

'If it's old mobile phones you want, we've got loads of them,' said Raffety, fascinated by Wonder's interest. 'Dr Braincrammer's banned them but everyone's got one. They're so cheap that people just chuck them away when the batteries go. I'm always digging them out of bins and recycling them in something.'

Wonder finished searching through Raffety's toolbox and before Raffety knew it, was taking the back off his computer.

'I hope you know what you're doing,' said Raffety nervously. 'The last time I did that, I couldn't put it back together again.'

As soon as he'd said it, Raffety felt like a fool. 'Of course he can. Wonder can fly – he can do anything!' he thought.

Raffety quickly realized that Wonder would need some kind of circuit board if he was going to fuse parts of his powerful home computer hard drive with the small computer already built into the old phone.

'Hey, let me do that,' said Raffety, ripping the back of one of his homemade toy robots. 'Do you need a wireless modem?'

'Mo-dem?' Wonder echoed.

'It's the device you need to connect to cyberspace. It works from practically anywhere.'

'Space,' said Wonder, nodding furiously. 'Wonder need modem.'

Two hours later, Raffety and Wonder had almost finished fusing the hard drive and modem onto the new circuit board.

'We need something to hold it all together,' said Raffety, realizing how jammed up the inner workings of his old phone now were.

He was just experimenting with various thicknesses of wire when there was a knock at the door.

'Raffety, the Chang family are here,' called

his mum. 'Come and say hello to Sky.'

'Play sick,' barked Wham.

'I'm too tired,' Raffety croaked, pushing his foot against the door.

'Raffety,' said Mrs Ray, in a familiar don't-you-mess-with-me tone.

'Don't worry, Mrs Ray,' Raffety heard Sky twitter. 'Raffety and I have already met. Perhaps he had a late night.'

'Crabite!' Raffety grunted quietly.

'Well if he did, he can tell his dad all about it later,' said Mrs Ray, pointedly.

'I'm sorry, Sky,' said Mrs Ray, lightening her tone. 'How about a mince pie?'

'That would be lovely, Mrs Ray.'

When he was sure that they were gone, Wonder began pushing keys on his interface before doing the same with Raffety's old phone.

'I think Wonder is trying to connect the computer inside my old phone with the computer on that baseship he showed me,' Raffety told Wham. Wham was impressed.

'Good boy,' he barked, wagging his tail.

When he was done, Wonder pointed Raffety's old phone right at him and pressed number 7. A beam of light shot from the phone and in an instant Raffety was invisible.

'So?' said Raffety, not realizing that anything had happened. He watched Wham run straight for him, crash into his leg and begin yapping like mad.

'What's the matter, Wham boy?' asked Raffety, feeling confused.

ARTWORK TO FOLLOW

Wham froze, boggle-eyed before him.

'He can't see me,' thought Raffety, feeling a tingle of excitement when he finally realized that Wham appeared to be staring right through him.

'I can make myself invisible to others but still see myself,' said Raffety, waving his hands before Wham's bewildered eyes. 'How cool is that?'

'You all right in there?' Mrs Ray called down the corridor.

'Yes, Mum,' Raffety shouted. 'It was only a spider.'

He looked to his fantabulous new toy. 'Can it zap?' he asked Wonder.

Wonder looked dumb.

Raffety pressed number 1 and accidently shot a red beam straight into Wonder's head.

KA-BOOM!

Wonder exploded into a trillion silver pixels.

'Ahhh!' Raffety screamed again.

He pressed it again, and to his relief Wonder instantly re-formed.

'Raffety!' Mr Ray shouted. 'Keep it down.'

'Wonder, are you all right?' Raffety whispered.

Wonder was running through a personal checklist of body parts and looking frazzled.

When he saw sure that Wonder was okay, Raffety then went from button to button trying to work out what everything did. On number 2 nothing seemed to happen but then by pressing it again Raffety found that he had recorded a really tedious video of the mess on the floor.

'Even ordinary phones in our world can do this,' Raffety said, sounding wholly unimpressed.

Raffety had no idea just how powerful such an apparently simple technical device would be, given the right situation. But like any boy eager to find flashy bang-crash-wallop features on a new toy, Raffety didn't pause to notice what happened at the press of each button.

'Half the buttons don't work,' he complained, feeling miffed that flying didn't seem to be an option. Despite this, Raffety was still pleased with his new toy. 'Of course – it's not finished yet,' he told himself. 'And just imagine what Zap Boy could do with a toy like this.'

'This toy has to have great name,' Raffety blurted out loud. He paused to rack his brain. 'It's like some kind of Wonder Toy... a, a, Zapper... a...' and then it came to him. '... a Wonder Zap-1.'

'Wonder Zap-1,' Wonder repeated.

'It's got to be number one because there's bound to be an update,' Raffety explained.

Raffety's mind started to explore the possibility of a toy that could make him invisible and zap things into zillions of particles. Suddenly he knew what he wanted to do. 'Minister Crabwitch will be in Kutan getting ready for her big speech...' he thought.

'I need to get to Kutan,' Raffety told Wonder, excitedly. He held out his Wonder Zap-1. 'Can this thing make me fly like you, Wonder?' he asked. 'Can it? Can it? Can it?' Raffety used his hands to help Wonder understand but there was no need. The alien was picking up Earth talk fast and by now understood almost everything. Wonder knew that, with one simple adjustment to the Wonder Zap, he could give Raffety flying powers through the device itself. The problem was the signal back to his baseship, which was sure to be intermittent given the amount of junk orbiting this exceptionally wasteful planet. Wonder considered his options. He looked first to Wham. 'The furry creature I can help,' he thought, considering again the transferral of some of his innate Uaan powers. 'But the Earthling might never have the mental capacity to control the powers.'

Unable to decide what to do for the best, Wonder chose to experiment. For option one, he made the simple adjustment to Raffety's Wonder Zap, creating a link to the computer on his baseship that would to enable Raffety to fly using the device – just as long as the signal was strong. Option two, however, was risky and much harder to pull off. If this option worked, Raffety and Wham would be able to fly, make themselves invisible and much more besides. And they wouldn't even need the Wonder Zap – as long as they could master and control their new powers. The great advantage of option two was that it didn't rely on the signal to Wonder's baseship because the powers were inside *them*.

Wonder flew up onto the bed and beckoned them both to sit down before him. Raffety dropped uneasily to his knees. He felt Wonder's fingers running through his hair. 'He can't be looking for nits,' he thought. 'Mum rubbed in all that gel.' Wonder fell into a trance.

KA-TUUUMMMM.

A sizzling shot of energy shook Wham and Raffety's bodies, and once again Raffety found his bedroom had turned into some fantastical virtual world.

'Ki-ako-ta-ki-aki...' Wonder began to sing, 'Ki-ta-ma-ma-ki-ta-le...'

'What's happening?' Raffety gasped nervously as he and his dog briefly became two dazzling stars of light.

With a vague feeling that he was about to be hung from the nearest Christmas tree, Raffety looked down. What he saw totally blew his mind.

WASTED POWERS

Initially, Wonder was very pleased. The transference of some of his Uaan powers to the Earthling and his dog had gone well. A few minutes later a bewildered Raffety Ray found himself flying through the bedroom window followed by a very panicky Wham.

'This is totally zaptastic!' Raffety gasped in astonishment, gazing up at a stunning night sky, for once free from cloud.

'Get me down!' howled Wham.

Raffety flapped his arms uselessly about his body until he realized that all he needed to do was focus on where he wanted to go.

'This is a comic book dream come true,' he cheered. 'I can fly and make myself invisible. I have zappers, a sidekick dog and a friend who's an alien – what else does a superhero need?'

As it turned out – a warm coat and a compass.

'Where are we?' Raffety shivered, five minutes later.

For Raffety and his gang to plot a route to Kutan and arrive in time to sabotage Crabwitch's 15:00 speech, Raffety needed to get his bearings fast. He looked down and saw the ruins of the old BBC studios.

'Kutan was built over Milton Keynes,' he told Wonder. 'It's north-west from here.'

With a little navigation theory that Raffety had crammed for a geography test, the gang set off on course. Unknown to Raffety and Wham, Wonder remained largely in control as he guided them through the early stages of their new flying power.

'Crabwitch won't see this coming,' Raffety shivered, already planning his next move. 'If we can make her look like a fool during her three o'clock speech at least kids everywhere will have something to smile about.'

It wasn't much. But it was something. An attempt at least to fight back.

Raffety soon discovered that he could change direction simply by leaning this way or that. As for speed, it seemed to depend on his willpower. This wasn't a problem for Raffety, but for Wham, who hated heights, his willpower was set very clearly on getting to the streets below.

'Next time I'm bringing a lead,' Raffety snapped, flying down to pull Wham up.

ROUGH PENCILS

Several minutes into the flight, Wonder noticed that although the signal to the baseship computer was temporarily blocked, effectively making the Wonder Zap useless, Raffety and Wham were flying well using the powers he had given them.

'Maybe I should have given the Earthling a little more credit,' he thought.

It was then that disaster struck. Raffety looked down and for a split second had a serious crisis in confidence. 'I must be dreaming,' he thought. 'I can't fly.'

Luckily, Raffety was flying only a few metres above a hill when he lost control of his new powers.

'What's happening?' he cried as he fell from the sky.

Crashing onto the grassy bank, he rolled until he bounced into a hedge.

'Ow,' he groaned, feeling battered and bruised all over.

He slowly got up and brushed himself down.

'What happened?' Raffety asked, turning to Wham and Wonder who had both landed with ease.

Wham bounded to the nearest tree while Wonder shrugged and sadly shook his head. 'It's as I thought,' he told himself. 'Uaan powers are wasted on this Earthling. He can't control his power.'

Needing a reason he could understand, Raffety looked up into the twinkling heavens and found one.

'There are so many moving satellites out there,' he muttered, taking in the sight of all the moving lights. 'Maybe all that space junk blocks the signal to your baseship.'

Although Raffety's logic was commendable, Wonder was still very disappointed to see how quickly Raffety could lose control of his new powers. 'Earthling needs to *imagine* himself flying,' Wonder told Raffety. 'Imagine it in your mind and it will be.'

But Raffety was too lost in his own thoughts to even hear, let alone understand Wonder's very important advice. Unaware of the miracle that had taken place in his bedroom, it was Raffety's belief that his powers were coming directly from the Wonder Zap-1 and the realization that it might have a serious glitch was both a shock and a worry. He decided to make his way to the top of the hill, hoping for a better signal and as it happened he got one. Using the power afforded him solely by the Wonder Zap-1, Raffety flapped and wobbled his way back into the sky, choosing to fly as close to the ground as possible.

Half an hour later, the monstrous towers of the National Power Station loomed out of the polluted sky over Kutan.

'The NPS is the biggest power station in the world,' Raffety told his gang.

In Dog World, Wham was really cheering up. He couldn't care less about the power station, – not with the new powers Wonder had given him. With no need of a Wonder Zap-1, Wham found he could control his own flying and invisibility powers at will. '*Now* put me in a yard with those pit bulls,' he was thinking. 'I'll show 'em.'

Flying over the Kutan Heaps on the outskirts of the city, Raffety saw many children hunting for food.

'Imagine if every child in the country got their hands on a Wonder Zap-1?' he thought. 'How fab would that be?'

A few minutes later, Raffety pointed to an enormous, black dome to the east of the power station. 'Kutan World,' he announced. 'Home to every politician and celebrity in the country.' It was also the home of Kutan Studios, where all the nation's programmes were made.

Raffety felt uneasy as they began to climb

higher to avoid the suburban rooftops and the whirring blades of the wind turbines. 'If the signal to Wonder's baseship fails now, I've had it,' he thought. But it was the racket made by the wind turbines that almost brought about their downfall.

'Yikes!' Raffety cried, as the helijet shot past. For a few seconds, the trail of smoke from the helijet's rockets blinded them.

'Ten metres closer and we'd have been dog meat for sure,' Raffety spluttered.

'Dinner?' barked Wham, looking around.

Raffety willed himself on. 'I bet that's Crabwitch's private jet,' he wheezed, 'Come on.'

As the helijet approached Kutan World, the dome opened like the petals of a huge Venus flytrap. The helijet hovered for a short while over the opening and then slowly began its descent.

Raffety checked his watch as the three intruders followed the helijet down to the helipad. '14:37,' he thought. 'There isn't much time.'

With the powers Wonder had given to Raffety and Wham, they were all able to see one another while remaining invisible to everyone else. Despite this, Raffety, who was yet to understand his powers, decided to give them all a quick number 7 invisibility zap with his Wonder Zap-1, just in case.

As he came down to land, Raffety saw Prime Minister Shrub, wearing a gold sequined suit, zooming across the red carpet on a spectacular hover-buggy.

'Where's Wham?' Raffety asked Wonder.

Wonder pointed to the large saucer of creamy milk by the landing pad.

'Typical,' Raffety tutted, seeing Wham was already lapping it up.

The helijet door swept open.

'Attention!' ordered the head guard.

Everyone stood up as the tall, skeletal figure of Minister Geerta Crabwitch, garbed in a tight metallic suit and boots, stepped out onto the red carpet and looked menacingly around.

Raffety shivered.

INTERGALACTIC
POWER LINK

'Flowers?' screeched Crabwitch, tossing away the bouquet Prime Minister Shrub proudly handed her. 'Where's the parade?'

'It's Christmas Day, Geerta, dear,' said the Prime Minister, meekly. 'The children are on holiday...'

Wham hadn't noticed the strange animal that followed Crabwitch out of the helijet.

'Wham – watch out!' Raffety hissed when he saw the terrifying, one-eyed cat charging straight towards his invisible dog.

'KA-CHAWWRRRRR,' spat the confused cat, pouncing wildly around the saucer. Wham

leapt back, his hair like a porcupine as heads everywhere turned to watch the cat's electric dance.

'Spite. Here. Now!' Crabwitch yelled. The cat leapt to her mistress's side but kept her evil-looking eye suspiciously focused on the spot where Wham stood shaking with fear.

A hefty black box was hauled onto the hover-buggy by Kutan security.

'What's that?' thought Raffety, sensing danger. Crabwitch reached inside her pocket for a fistful of talc and rubbed it into her sweaty hands. Inspecting the heliport with fierce eyes, she finally got onto the buggy herself.

'Away!' she shrieked.

'After her!' Raffety urged his gang. And off they flew.

Raffety thought Kutan World was the coolest place he'd ever seen. Flying through the first opening door, his little gang found themselves over a stunning tropical beach lined with cafes and restaurants, where many residents were relaxing in the simulated sunshine. At a junction with signs to private apartments and studios, the Prime Minister's buggy surprisingly turned towards the apartments.

'I thought Crabwitch would be heading straight for the studios,' thought Raffety, unaware how close the elite apartments were to the studios.

Zooming after the Prime Minister's buggy the gang were halfway down a wide corridor lined with exotic plants when it stopped outside a door marked 'VIP Apartment'. Two crow-faced guards stood to attention outside as Minister Crabwitch got out.

'In!' Raffety hissed as the door swished open.

Crabwitch waved a dismissive hand at the

Prime Minister, grabbed the black box and stormed inside. With Spite at her heels, Crabwitch slammed her hand on the electric door pad and twenty locks clunked shut.

'We're trapped,' Raffety shuddered, terrified to think that his invisibility powers could be blocked at any time by a big clump of space junk.

The gang huddled by the door while Crabwitch dimmed the lights and closed the automated blinds. One of the slats was broken, exposing a tiny needle of moonlight.

'Time to open the intergalactic power link,' Crabwitch cackled.

She cracked her bony fingers and with stilt-like strides, crossed the room and lifted the large black box up onto the table.

'How about a hundred thousand kilowatt-hours of electricity, Spite?' Crabwitch crowed. 'Let's see what Uaan-4 makes of that when the Zheta battlestar fires on them.'

Wonder flopped to the ground by Raffety's feet, his face etched in stress while Crabwitch scooped up another fistful of talc and rubbed it into her sweaty hands and forehead.

'What's going on here?' thought Raffety, sensing that somehow Wonder's mission on Earth was linked to Crabwitch.

They watched Crabwitch pressed a sequence of buttons and then opened the box to reveal a console packed with dials, knobs and big chunky levers. With Wonder and Wham trembling against his legs, Raffety tried to imagine what the console might do.

He soon found out.

Crabwitch reached inside the box, yanked out a big clump of cable and bellowed: *'Zi-ta-ku-ta!'*

The cable shot from her hands, throwing up a cloud of talcum powder, and began to uncoil like a snake. Raffety gasped and Crabwitch and Spite instantly turned around. 'They're looking right at us,' Raffety shuddered, terrified to see the fine particles of talc that had settled on his arms.

'Arachnacams!' Crabwitch shouted. 'Get 'em Spite.'

The invisible onlookers sighed with relief to

see two arachnacams scuttling to the air vent. Spite pounced, crushing them in seconds into a mush of wires and metal.

'*A-ki-ka!*' Crabwitch shrieked.

Many smaller leads then sprang from the main cable and began to plug themselves into electric sockets all over the room.

'She really is a witch,' Raffety shuddered.

'*Hi-tu!*'

A monitor jerked up from the back of the console.

Wonder clasped Raffety's leg so hard it hurt.

'*Ki-ta-hi,*' Crabwitch screeched.

The face of a ferocious creature burst onto the monitor – its burning red flesh and Cyclops eye so repugnant that the three intruders were forced to turn away.

'She's communicating with aliens!' Raffety trembled. 'And they don't look as friendly as Wonder.' Suddenly Raffety's notion that he was simply going to play a little prank and write a few graffiti slogans felt truly pathetic.

'Crabwitch to NPS Control,' the Minister

blurted out, abruptly reverting to English. The monitor switched to split-screen, showing both Crabwitch's alien contact and a gaunt human teenager in a smart grey uniform.

'Yes, Minister,' trembled the spotty youth.

'Prepare to open intergalactic power link to the Zheta battlestar. The deadline for power transfer is upon us.'

Raffety's heart was pounding so hard it hurt.

Crabwitch slammed her hands down onto two metal pads on the console.

'Commence countdown: 10, 9, 8...'

'What's happening?' Raffety panicked.

'...ZERO.'

There was an eruption of light, an ear-deafening buzz and Crabwitch and Spite went into violent spasm.

'Danger, danger...' Wonder was gasping. 'Must stop, must stop.'

He leapt onto the main cable and started to pull.

'We've got company!' Crabwitch squealed.

Then the room went black.

CRABWITCH
EXPOSED

'What are you doing?' Raffety cried.

Wonder was tugging hard at the cable while Crabwitch scanned the room with laser-red eyes. 'Who are you?' Crabwitch screamed, staring straight through them.

Then Wham jumped onto the console and began pawing willy-nilly at the buttons and levers. As cables writhed and sparks shot from Crabwitch's body, there were loud bangs from the door.

Crabwitch jerked away from the controls and the power surge stopped.

'Lights,' she shouted. 'Show yourselves!'

The three intruders were quivering in the dark with fear. 'We're so fried,' thought Raffety. 'There's no way out.'

Suddenly the door was blasted open, filling the room with blinding light and smoke. As the security guards rushed in, Raffety scooped up Wonder, grabbed Wham's collar and pelted for the door.

'Cretins!' Crabwitch spluttered to the guards. She followed the moving shapes in the smoke as they disappeared through the door. 'Uaans,' she muttered through gritted teeth, 'with those cursed invisibility powers, I knew it!'

When they were safely away, Raffety turned to his gang.

'Wonder, are you OK?' he panted.

Wonder's face was etched with pain. Sounds came pouring from his mouth, some in English, some not. Wham understood every word and Raffety pieced together what he could.

'Empress Ogoron,' Wham translated to himself. 'Leader of the Zheta. Sworn enemy of the Uaan Race.'

Wonder looked as grey as a squirrel.

'So Crabwitch is an alien too?' Raffety gasped, trying to compute the scale of their terrifying discovery. 'And she's using power from the NPS to do something really bad – I know it.'

'The Zheta will use Earth power to destroy Uaan-4. No Uaan-4, no Wonder.' Wham was wide-eyed at Wonder's words.

'She wants to destroy your baseship, Wonder,' Raffety gasped. 'That's why you're here.' He quickly checked his watch. 'It's less than five minutes to Crabwitch's broadcast on national TV. Let's do what we can to weaken her control in this world, right here, right now.'

Against a racket of sirens and guards charging uselessly about, Raffety led his invisible gang to Studio One where a big Christmas banquet buffet was laid out before the cameras and a large, leather-bound throne.

'I tell you, there are rebels in the building right now!' Crabwitch was screaming at the Prime Minister. 'We have to hunt them down. Strengthen the Wall. Triple the guard. This attack must not be tolerated.'

But there was no time for Crabwitch to calm down. Her attempt to divert power back to the Zheta battleship had failed and she was fuming. As the cameras moved in and Crabwitch was ushered to her throne, Raffety noticed the timid young make-up girl, too terrified to approach. He flew across, grabbed a fistful of lipsticks and soared to the white wall behind Crabwitch's throne. Above her head, while the floor manager began his final countdown, Raffety scrawled out the words:

Crabwitch is an alien

Before Crabwitch knew it, she was live on national TV, looking wild, wicked and enraged.

'Well, comrades, another Christmas is here...' Crabwitch began, with smoke wafting from her ears.

'Now! Now! Now!' yapped Wham from his hiding-place under the table. 'You've got to do something NOW!'

Raffety had just finished scrawling *Down With Braincramming* and *Time 4 Play* onto the set when he looked down at Crabwitch's huge, wiry wig. 'What's she hiding?' he thought. Quick as a flash, he flew down, grabbed huge fistfuls of 'hair' and tugged with all his might.

'Get off me!' Crabwitch yelled as she and her static-infused wig flew into raging fit. Now smoke was billowing from her ears, nose *and* mouth, and huge clumps of hair appeared to jettison from the Minister's hairpiece.

'Her wig's coming off,' someone gasped.

That was all the encouragement Raffety needed. With one final yank, the whole wig came off in his hands, revealing a hideous green-veined scalp beneath.

'We're under attack,' Crabwitch roared. 'Cut the cameras. Call up the National Guard. Hunt the rebels down.'

Spite leapt up onto Crabwitch's head in an effort to hide the revelation while Raffety made a swoop for the food. 'Come on,' he called to his friends. 'Grab as much as you can. Then we're off to the Heaps.'

Suddenly, Geerta Crabwitch stood still, glaring at one of the TV screens. Wonder followed her eyes and saw to his horror, the faint, reflected outline of his otherwise invisible body amid the smoke.

'Close all the exits!' Crabwitch ordered.

Raffety pulled Wham away from a raspberry trifle.

'Let's get out of here!' he cried.

THE FIGHT BACK BEGINS

Raffety, Wham and Wonder flew at jet speed through the corridors and up through the closing roof of the helipad just in time.

'We did it, we did it,' Raffety cheered, as they flew towards London with a tablecloth 'sack' filled with stolen treats. 'Crabwitch will be the laughing stock of the whole nation.'

Raffety's mind was turning faster than the turbines around him, propelling him home with a brilliant idea.

When they arrived at the Heaps, there was an atmosphere of celebration.

'Did you see the speech?' cheered Anna Polanski excitedly, running to greet them. 'We manage to record it before they shut the network down.'

Crabwitch's embarrassment was being repeated endlessly on every monitor Raffety could see.

'They're saying that the rebels set the whole thing up to make Minister Crabwitch look like a freak,' said Anna.

Raffety felt gutted. 'Then they've managed to cover the whole thing up,' he thought, feeling more determined than ever to expose Crabwitch for who she really was.

The eyes of all the children in the Heaps lit up when they saw the food Raffety had brought with him.

'We haven't eaten food like this for years,' said Anna, beaming with joy.

Leaving the party food for the children to share, Raffety took Anna to one side. He examined her kind, determined eyes. 'This is so dangerous,' he thought, hesitant that he was doing the right thing. 'But she's so brave and I really do need her help.'

'Anna,' he started, as sternly as he'd ever said anything his whole life. 'What I'm about to show you must remain a secret, and go no further than you and your most trusted friends.'

Anna looked puzzled but nodded slowly. Raffety took a deep breath. 'Wonder,' he sighed. 'Can you please show yourself to my friend.'

Anna's jaw dropped when Wonder appeared.

Then Raffety told Anna everything. All about Wonder and the Wonder Zap-1 and what it could do, and how Crabwitch was really an alien called Empress Ogoron, leader of the Zheta and sworn enemy of Wonder's Uaan race. He told her how Crabwitch was drawing power from the National Power Station to fuel an attack on Wonder's baseship, Uaan-4 – he told her everything!

'So that's why she's so desperate to control everything,' said Anna, her eyes burning with rage. 'That's why the coal mines beyond the Wall are so important to her and why there's so little electricity left for anything else.'

'If we're going to expose her, our fight back will need hard drives, modems, mobile phones and every battery and charger you can find,' Raffety told Anna. 'I need you to spread this news to children across every Heap in the country. The more children we have with a Wonder Zap-1, the more chance we have to bring Crabwitch down. If we can expose her as an alien, Prime Minister Shrub will have to get rid of her. And then we can start making demands of our own.'

'We could get rid of Braincramming and Correction School,' said Anna excitedly.

'And rescue all the children working in the coal mines beyond the wall,' said Raffety.

They paused to consider the importance of what they wanted to achieve.

'But who shall we say is leading the fight?' asked Anna, thoughtfully.

Raffety considered this for a moment.

'Zap Boy,' he replied, proudly. 'Tell them to hack onto the hyperweb and visit the Zap Boy blog.'

Raffety suddenly noticed that Wonder had wandered away and was looking anxiously at his console.

'He can't get a signal home,' Raffety muttered.

And it was true. For while Wonder required no signal home to enable him to do all kinds of things, communicating with his baseship was sometimes impossible.

'And he's so far from home and his family and friends,' said Anna sympathetically. But she paused for only a moment. Now was the time for action.

Raffety was already getting to work. He grabbed some cardboard and something to write with and drew a diagram of the basic Wonder Zap. He then wrote some notes on which type of mobile phones worked best, which computer chips and wireless modems needed to be inserted, and a whole list of instructions on how to build a Wonder Zap.

'You'll have to collect as many of these resources as you can and then train the children how to make them,' he told her. 'Wonder will show you how to log all the Wonder Zaps onto the computer on his baseship.' Raffety paused. 'There is one thing I have to warn you about.' Anna looked worried. Raffety looked up into the sky and continued. 'Sometimes all that space junk up there collides and blocks the signal between here and Wonder's baseship.'

'And then nothing works,' said Anna, frowning, 'and we're completely exposed.'

Raffety nodded slowly, then, turning to Wonder. 'Let's keep it simple. Forget flying, it's too dangerous. Just program an invisibility setting in all the new Wonder Zap-1s – that's enough for now.'

Leaving Wonder with Anna and the children to begin mass-production of the Wonder Zap-1, Raffety and Wham headed through the grey skies for home.

As they flew swiftly on through the fading afternoon light, it wasn't just the rapidly falling temperature that made Raffety shiver.

'What have I started?' he trembled to

himself. 'Crabwitch is an alien Empress who can draw on incredible powers. She'll never rest until she's tracked us all down and obliterated us from the planet.'

Raffety Ray could not have been more right.

BARMY TOWERS

It was late afternoon on Christmas Day and the streets and sky were dense with police helijets and cruisers. Raffety and Wham were almost home when they heard Mr and Mrs Ray calling for them.

'Back me up,' Raffety told Wham as they landed by the bins. Raffety zapped himself visible using the Wonder Zap and was surprised when it appeared Wham had already done the same.

'There's Wham!' shouted Mr Ray, running over.

'How did you do that?' Raffety muttered to Wham as he too stepped into view.

'Where have you been?' Mrs Ray cried with

relief when she saw them. 'The country is under attack.' She paused in disbelief at the state of Raffety's appearance. 'And what have you done with your coat?'

'I took Wham for a walk,' Raffety lied.

'Don't listen to him,' Wham yapped.

'Some horrible pit bulls attacked us and Wham bolted,' Raffety went on. 'It took me ages to find him.'

'Is that trifle on Wham's face?' asked Mr Ray, peering down.

'Whipped away right under my nose,' Wham grumbled, licking his chops.

Having missed Christmas dinner with Grandpa Ray and Aunty May, Mrs Ray warmed Raffety's dinner up in the zapper and he took it to his room. Hacking onto the hyperweb news, Raffety heard all about the rebel attack on Kutan Studios.

'Minister Crabwitch is a hero,' Prime Minster Shrub announced at the press conference. 'She fought the rebels off single-handedly.'

'We really rattled her,' thought Raffety

proudly. 'She's trying to cover everything up but we're on to her.'

Raffety called Wonder and Anna Polanski at the Heaps using his Wonder Zap-1. 'I'll come to the Heaps straight after school tomorrow,' he told them. Then he zonked out on the bed.

That night, while Raffety slept, Anna Polanski organized her gang into working groups, following Raffety's diagram and instructions to start production of the Wonder Zap-1.

'This is our secret,' Anna told the children. 'We are going to work with Zap Boy and Wonder to change our world.'

The next morning, Raffety awoke to the 6:00 siren.

'Time for school, Raffety, dear,' he heard his mum call.

For once, Raffety couldn't wait. He got dressed, slipped his Wonder Zap-1 into his pocket and dashed to the kitchen.

'See you later,' he told Wham through a mouthful of toast.

'Yeah, right,' Wham muttered, burying his

head under his pillow.

'Don't forget Sky,' called Mrs Ray as Raffety stormed out of the front door. 'I told Mrs Chang that you'd walk her to school.'

'No chance,' thought Raffety.

But Sky Chang was waiting right outside the front door.

'Morning.'

Raffety froze. 'Crabites!' he said to himself.

Sky looked very smart in her grey school uniform and well-polished boots.

'Where's your coat?' asked Sky. 'It's cold and rainy out.'

'Coats are for wimps,' said Raffety.

He started to run.

'Can you show me the way, please?' Sky begged, running after him. 'It *is* my first day.'

Raffety groaned and slowed down.

'Hey,' said Sky, excitedly. 'Did you see Minister Crabwitch lose her wig on national TV?'

'Yeah,' said Raffety, trying to hide his scorn. 'I thought she was very brave. What with all those invisible rebels and everything.'

'Invisible!' Sky exclaimed. 'They didn't mention *that* on the news.'

'Oh,' Raffety fumbled. 'I just meant we didn't get to see them on the TV.'

Barmy Towers School was said to be a masterpiece of modern architecture. Built using enormous blocks of concrete, its rectangular design and immense towers depressed every child forced to go there.

'It suggests the notion that our brains are like a box,' Mr Ray had lectured Raffety on the artistic merits of the building. 'We should think only inside them, and fill them with as many facts as we can. Quite brilliant!'

Most children felt sick when they saw the gargoyle-clad walls for the first time. The barred windows and doors were supposedly there to protect the hi-tech facilities inside but that wasn't how it felt. Following his obsession with parts of the brain, Dr Braincrammer called the classrooms 'cells'. Each was dimly lit by naked low-watt bulbs and crammed with computerized workstations.

That morning, the high-fenced holding cage outside was crammed with children whipped into a frenzy by yesterday's wigless revelations on TV.

'Crabwitch is a freak,' Jake Harrison whispered to Raffety. 'My dad actually laughed at her.' He quickly looked around. 'But only for a second,' he added, warily.

The school doors opened and Raffety's eyes shot to the detention board.

'Ow!' He flinched when he saw that his name was flashing red at the top of the list with forty-eight detentions.

Looming above the detention board was the hologram of Crabwitch's infamous, potholed face. Her granite-like glare, crooked nose and jagged jaw, which appeared to loom over school lobbies all over the country, would have presented a terrifying challenge for an experienced abseiler, let alone an impressionable child.

'Raffety Ray!'

Raffety squealed with shock as Dr Braincrammer leapt from the shadows. 'My office. Now!'

Within seconds, Raffety had been bundled into the dark, laboratory-like world of Dr Braincrammer's office.

'It's come to my attention, you ginger-haired squirt,' Braincrammer yelled, 'that not only have you broken the 24-hour world record for ASBOs, but you were out walking your scrappy little mongrel when you should have been at home watching Minister Crabwitch's speech.'

'Wham needed a walk,' Raffety quivered, his hand hovering over his Wonder Zap-1. 'He gets really agitated when he needs to pee.'

'Agitated?' cried Braincrammer. 'I'll show you agitated.'

Dr Braincrammer was seething with rage.

'Yes, sir,' Raffety croaked, withering at the sight of the brainfrazzler on Dr Braincrammer's desk.

'And I'm going to be keeping a very close eye on *everything* you get up to. Is that understood?'

'Yes, sir,' Raffety mumbled.

'Speak up.'

'Yes, sir.'

Raffety's first lesson was Chindi grammar in cell 481 with Ratakata Sticklash. Ms Sticklash was nearly two metres tall and as skinny as a stick. Her mousy hair was chestnut brown, but she had horrible white whiskers that sprouted from her ears, nose and chin. The children called her 'The Weasel', although no one could remember if the cage of rats and stoats that she kept in a cage on her desk arrived before or after her nickname was born.

'The Weasel eats rats for lunch,' Jake Harrison had muttered once. Unfortunately for Jake, the microphone at his desk had relayed his comment straight to Braincrammer's computer and within seconds he'd been called to the Head's office. By the time Braincrammer had used his brainfrazzler on Jake, he had returned to class needing a bib.

'Workstations on,' Sticklash commanded that morning. 'All the factoids for today's lesson can by found on the TLC website, page 6,432.'

Raffety peered through the gloom at the rows and rows of depressed children, sitting at their computers in their windowless cell. 'Can we really make enough Wonder Zaps to change all this?' he wondered.

Luckily, Raffety's first detention after school with Dr Braincrammer didn't involve electrical appliances but a 20-page exam on school policies.

* * *

'How are you, Wham, boy?' said Raffety, greeting Wham by the school gates at 18:07.

'Knackered,' Wham panted. Wham had been scavenging for old robotic toys all day. 'That alien is working me like a...' But Raffety was already flying away.

'You never listen to me,' Wham howled, launching himself after him.

They arrived at the Heaps just as the 18:30 curfew siren sounded.

Raffety found Wonder in the children's den, slumped against a pile of old phones and computers.

'He's exhausted,' said Anna. 'I'm making him some soup.'

'These Wonder Zaps are fantastic,' gushed a small boy, holding one up.

'There were two police raids today and we

just zapped ourselves right out of sight,' said Anna, happily.

'But it doesn't always work,' grumbled one of the older girls. 'I nearly got caught because suddenly the whole thing went wrong and I could be seen.'

'I know,' said Raffety, relieved that he had decided to program only the invisibility setting into the mass-produced Wonder Zap-1s.

'That could be dangerous,' said Anna,

looking concerned. 'It's no good being invisible one minute and then completely exposed the next.'

'That's why my Wonder Zap is the only one for now that's programmed with a "fly" option,' said Raffety.

'But just think what we could all do with an invisibility setting that works. How many have you made?'

'Over a hundred,' said Anna, distracted for a moment by a movement in the shadows. 'It's the best we could do.'

'Then we must help kids all over the country make their own at home,' said Raffety, who had been thinking about this all day. 'I can work with Wonder to make a hyperlink to the computer on his baseship. We can post it on the Zap Boy blog along with all the instructions and the software.'

'But our enemies will find it,' said Anna, distractedly, as yet again her eyes were drawn to something moving in the darkness.

'Wonder,' said Raffety, kneeling down by his tired friend. 'Can the computer on your baseship identify the age of anyone logging on?' A glassy-eyed Wonder nodded, just enough to give Raffety hope. 'And can your computer block adults accessing Wonder Zap powers?' asked Raffety.

Again, Wonder nodded.

'Then that's what we need to do,' cheered Raffety.

In their excitement none of them noticed the freakish, one-eyed cat that slipped quietly away into the night.

DISASTER STRIKES

Straight after supper, Raffety was back in his bedroom, beavering away at his blog.

'Nearly two thousands hits!' he cheered, when he checked his Zap Boy blog on the hyperweb.

Raffety guessed that most of these hits came from children living in and around Heaps all over the country.

'At least we're giving the children who most need it a chance to fight back,' Raffety told Wonder. 'If we all work together we can expose Crabwitch as an evil alien and stop her using Earth's power to strengthen the Zheta battlestar.

Your baseship might still have a chance of defending itself.'

Raffety and Wonder worked through the night on the instructions and software that would enable children everywhere to transform their ordinary phones into Wonder Zap-1s.

'Wonder has written in a code to make Wonder Zap-1 self-destruct when held by an Earthling adult,' Wonder told Raffety.

'Wonder, you're a genius!' Raffety exclaimed. With a clear signal to Wonder's baseship in space, Raffety used a hyperlink from the Zap Boy blog so that children everywhere could access the unique invisibility powers of Wonder's alien race.

'As soon as adults log onto the baseship computer, let's crash their computers with an overload of spam,' Raffety suggested as he began programming the software.

By 05:00 they were finished and Raffety closed down the computer.

'You're the best thing that ever happened to me,' Raffety told Wonder.

But Wonder wasn't listening. Again he was using his console to project a 3-D image of his baseship and star-fighters into the bedroom.

'You miss home, don't you?' said Raffety.

Even with his sunglasses on, Wonder could not hide his tears.

After a while, Raffety left Wonder to gaze at images from another world and crashed out on the bed. 'Wonder and I come from such different worlds,' he pondered. 'And yet we have so many things in common. Even our enemy.' He fell asleep trying to think of an idea that would help Wonder get home.

An hour later, Mrs Ray had to fight her way into Raffety's room.

'Raffety, wake up,' she pleaded, throwing all Raffety's toys and designs into a large plastic bin. 'The Channel 1 News is saying that Minister Crabwitch has ordered the biggest police hunt of all time. Any toy, anywhere, without an official TLC logo means instant prison for parents and Correction School for the kid.'

Raffety was suddenly wide awake. 'She's

tracking me down,' he thought.

He got up quickly and dressed, slipped his Wonder Zap-1 into his pocket and helped his mum. When all his toys were cleared away, Mrs Ray turned to Raffety's computer.

'I wasn't born yesterday,' she said, slipping it under her arm. 'If they find out you've been surfing the hyperweb you'll be in big trouble.'

'Wonder, are you here?' Raffety whispered after his mum had gone.

Raffety heard a faint snoring sound from under the bed and peered down.

'He's too tired to go anywhere,' thought Raffety, giving Wonder's head a gentle stroke.

When Raffety got to school and saw the car park jammed full of Ministry vehicles his heart sank. But then it got worse.

'Spite!' Raffety shuddered, seeing the one-eyed cat spying down from the roof. Raffety knew that the best way of protecting Zap Boy was by keeping his everyday disguise. If he used the Wonder Zap to make himself invisible now, it would be as incriminating as being caught red-handed with it. Raffety heard a call coming in on his Wonder Zap but there was no time to answer. 'If they take a register and I'm invisible, they'll hunt me down,' he panicked as he chucked it under a bin. But Raffety Ray wasn't the only pupil at Barmy Towers dumping incriminating evidence.

The morning siren went off and Dr Braincrammer's voice boomed over the tannoy.

'Into class lines. Now!'

As the children pushed and shoved themselves into regimented lines, the holding cage was quickly surrounded by Kutan Security. The school doors clanked opened and Dr Braincrammer marched out. Standing before the assembled school, Dr Braincrammer cleared his throat and began:

'The hunt for the rebels who attacked Minister Crabwitch on Christmas Day has led the authorities right here.' There were gasps of astonishment across the school.

'He's had a tip off,' thought Raffety, looking around for Sky Chang.

'This morning's house raids have already proved that some of you have been hacking onto illegal websites,' Braincrammer continued.

One boy on the front row fainted and was whisked away by two burly guards.

'Now,' Braincrammer went on. 'Whether you've been playing computer games, downloading comics or even...' Braincrammer paused to shake his head, 'reading the blog of a wanted felon known as Zap Boy...' Raffety felt his knees begin to sag, '... be prepared for a long stint in Correction School.'

One girl squealed and made a mad dash for the gate, only to be dragged away by guards.

'Good job Mum totally cleared my room,' thought Raffety. 'If they'd got the computer, they'd know everything.'

There was a crack of lightning followed by a roll of thunder.

'That's all we need,' thought Raffety, 'Another electrical storm.'

Then, through the darkening sky, Raffety saw the blast of helijet rockets.

'Crabwitch!' he shuddered. 'I should have zapped myself away when I had the chance.'

Again, Raffety looked around for Sky Chang, convinced that somehow she had something to do with all this.

Everyone in the holding cage looked up in dread as the helijet landed on the school roof and Crabwitch stepped out. Seconds later, she stormed into the cage, her hair, eyes, arms – everything – wild with rage.

'When will you pathetic children realize that play-toys mush your brain,' she screamed. 'You must live in the real world. Work hard. Cram facts. This government will not allow you to IMAGINE!'

Crabwitch began her careful inspection accompanied by Dr Braincrammer and his compuboard. Child by child. Line by line. Crabwitch glared into the eyes of each child while Braincrammer read salient facts from their records and guards frisked each of the children.

Five children up the line from Raffety, Crabwitch was grilling Jake Harrison.

'Name?'

'Harrison.'

'Age?'

'Twelve.'

'Who is Zap Boy?'

Suddenly Jake's eyes shot to Raffety Ray. 'I hope it works,' he shrieked, thrusting his hand into his pocket. The guards pounced on Jake and grabbed his phone.

'What's this?' Crabwitch squealed, as she

took the smouldering handset.

'It's just my phone,' Harrison blurted as he was dragged away.

As Geerta Crabwitch came face to face with Raffety Ray, the gathering black clouds finally blotted out the sun. Raffety felt something warm brush up against his leg. He looked down but saw nothing.

'Name?'

'Raffety Ray.'

Crabwitch paused to examine Raffety's profile while Dr Braincrammer consulted his compuboard.

'Sixteen ASBOs and away from home on Christmas afternoon,' Braincrammer read.

'I was walking my dog,' said Raffety.

'So you have a dog,' said Crabwitch, curiously. 'Interesting.'

Raffety scrutinized the Minister's craggy, potholed skin. 'It's more like the lunar surface than skin,' he concluded, hunting for the seams of her disguise. Raffety was sure that there was an alien in there somewhere.

'Clean, ma'am,' said the guard when he'd frisked Raffety down.

'*Clean*?' Crabwitch squealed. 'He's filthy. Especially his brain. Rats know more facts than he does.' She turned to Raffety. 'Your card is marked, boy,' she growled. 'There's no hiding from me. I have eyes everywhere. Isn't that right, Spite?'

Raffety felt a sharp, painful clawing at his shins.

'Get off!' he snapped, shaking Spite off his leg.

'There's a note here that the boy's flat was raided first thing this morning,' said Braincrammer. Raffety's heart sank. 'Apparently his mother was arrested.'

Raffety had a suicidal impulse to run.

A guard marched up to Crabwitch and saluted.

'We've discovered sixteen suspect phones in and around the school bins alone, Minister,' he announced.

Suddenly, Spite leapt away and began

pawing madly, seemingly at mid-air.

'That's it, Spite – hold it down!' Crabwitch bellowed.

Crabwitch reached into her pockets, lurched towards Spite and threw a big handful of talc into the air.

'The crazy cat is having a fit,' thought Raffety as children quickly shuffled back to get away from Spite's wild, clawing paws.

But as the talc started to settle, Raffety saw to his horror the faint outline of another creature – one he recognized at once.

'Stand back!' Crabwitch yelled.

Suddenly a huge of bolt of green lightning appeared to shoot from her outstretched finger, creating an instant force field around the terrified creature trapped inside.

'No!!!' Raffety screamed.

He made a move to run to Wonder's aid but was tripped up and forced down with a boot.

'Let me go!' Raffety wheezed.

Inside the force field Wonder's whole body could be seen, illuminated in a throbbing green

silhouette cast by the electrified bars of his prison.
As the rain began, Crabwitch guided her prisoner
surrounded by the force field through the crowd
of horrified children and up into her helijet.

The boot on Raffety's back finally lifted and
he turned around to see Sky Chang glaring down.

Raffety hauled himself up and got right up to
her face.

'You snitched on us,' he snarled.

Sky Chang didn't even flinch.

Raffety pushed her hard away.

Turned on his heels.

And ran.

DOWN IN
THE DUMPS

Raffety pelted through the storm, his heart throbbing, his mind in chaos. 'Wonder must have come to tell me about the raid on the flat and Mum's arrest,' he thought. Raffety knew that he couldn't return home, so he headed for the Heaps.

He found Anna Polanski in the hideout where hundreds of children were working hard to make Wonder Zaps for children in the suburbs who couldn't get to a computer.

'None of the Wonder Zaps work,' she told Raffety, peering anxiously at his deranged appearance. 'There's no signal.' She handed Raffety one of the latest Wonder Zaps. Raffety put it into his pocket and took Anna to one side.

'So what are you going to do?' she asked him, after Raffety had told her everything.

'Maybe Crabwitch took Wonder back to Kutan,' said Raffety. 'I'll have to fly back there somehow.'

Exhausted, and at a loss as to how he was going to get to Kutan, Raffety stumbled out into the storm, finally collapsing onto a soggy pile of rubbish.

'This really is the end,' he thought as he lay on his back and closed his eyes.

Raffety had no idea how long he lay there trying to process everything that had happened. But somehow, through the confusion in his mind, he started to piece together little snippets of memory that, when put together, started to create a crazy idea.

'Just before I flew for the first time,' he thought, 'Wonder went into a trance, and me and Wham turned into incredibly bright stars...' Raffety pulled himself up. '...When I had a moment's doubt that I could fly, I fell from the sky while Wham just carried on.' Raffety had thought at the time that his fall had had something to do with space junk blocking the signal to Wonder's baseship.

'Wham doesn't even need a Wonder Zap-1,' he said out loud. 'What if that's the same with me?'

Raffety scrambled up to the top of a huge pile of rubbish and looked out through the storm-ravaged sky. As he quickly scanned his memory, it finally struck him that he'd never really asked Wonder what had actually happened during that strange act he'd performed on him and Wham just before their flight to Kutan.

'There must have been some sort of power transfer,' he thought. 'But how does it work?' He bent his knees and launched himself up – and landed flat on his face in the rubbish. Standing up and brushing himself down, Raffety again thought back over that flight to Kutan. 'Wonder said something,' he recalled. 'Something about how I had to *imagine* myself flying.'

'I have the power,' he muttered. 'I don't need

the Wonder Zap.' Suddenly the exact phrase popped into his mind: 'Imagine it in your mind and it will be.' Raffety closed his eyes.

He imagined being able to fly with such focus and concentration that in his mind he actually saw himself soaring into the sky. Then he clenched his fists, bent his knees and jumped, stretching his arms out high above his head, just as he had pictured Zap Boy doing in every homemade comic he'd every drawn.

This time, when Raffety opened his eyes, he really was flying – high above the Heaps.

'It works!' he cried out loud. 'I *am* Zap Boy!'

THE MOMENT
OF TRUTH

Seeing the children on the ground, Raffety thought himself invisible and swooped down over their heads.

'I *am* Zap Boy!'

Heads below looked bewilderedly up into the sky. They could see nothing unusual, yet just hearing Zap Boy's voice somehow filled them with hope.

Raffety Ray knew enough about super-heroes to know that he could never reveal his true identify to the world. 'Secrecy is a weapon in itself,' he reminded himself.

Unlike in his homemade comics, Raffety's

transformation to Zap Boy wasn't glamorous. There was no fancy costume, and he was freezing and soaking wet. But Raffety Ray was suddenly filled with hope. Just then, he saw Wham flying up towards him and within seconds they were reunited.

'About time,' woofed Wham.

'Wham, we're going to Kutan to rescue Wonder,' Zap Boy announced. This time, Zap Boy and Wham flew at supersonic speed, and minutes later were circling Kutan World, looking through window after window as they hunted for Crabwitch's apartment. Zap Boy was just flying past a window with its blind drawn when he noticed a tiny chink in the slats.

'Here, boy,' he called to Wham.

Wham flew over and together they peered through.

'HA-WOO,' howled Wham, wincing with fear at the sight of a poor, defenceless Wonder, crammed up inside a slowly contracting force field.

'This is pure evil,' Zap Boy gasped. 'The

force field is too strong for him. His powers are useless against it.'

Crabwitch and Spite were again connected to the console and convulsing through a huge surge of electricity.

'We've got to stop them now!' Zap Boy cried. 'Before Wonder is squished.'

Zap Boy pulled out his Wonder Zap-1, pressed number 1 and fired straight at the window.

ZA-BOOMM!

The window shattered into a billion particles. Crabwitch, startled by the explosion, turned to the window as a strong, cold wind blasted through her wig. She yanked her hands from the box and the force field around Wonder instantly dulled.

'Show yourselves!' she yelled, her eyes fired with rage.

But Zap Boy had no intention of lowering his guard. He shot over to the force field and again fired a number 1 zap, this time at the cable that linked it to Crabwitch's black box.

ZA-BOOM!

One zap with the Wonder Zap-1 and the force field faltered just long enough for Wonder to jump from his electrified prison. Spite leapt from Crabwitch's side as Wonder squealed in terror and shot to an air vent in the wall. Ripping the bars off with his bare paws, Wonder scampered into the vent, followed by a ferociously hissing Spite.

A blaring siren forced Zap Boy to slam his hands over his ears.

'The whole place will be surrounded in seconds,' Crabwitch bellowed. 'There's no escape.'

Zap Boy turned around and nearly screamed. There before him, scaling up, up, up into the roof of the room, was Crabwitch, shedding clothes, hair, skin – everything – as her Earthly disguise began to fall away, revealing the first hints of the dazzling metallic creature beneath.

'She's transforming herself to destroy me!' Zap Boy gasped.

He stretched out his arms and shot at her with his Wonder Zap but nothing fired. He fired again and again and again, holding his aim firm but each time there was no response from his Wonder Zap. He looked anxiously to his hand and saw that his trembling finger had been pressing down on a 2 and not 1. He quickly moved his finger to a 1 and fired.

KA-BOOM!

A red laser beam of light shot from his Wonder Zap. But by now Empress Ogoron was almost fully transformed into the huge, robot-like creature that was her true form, her burning eyes blistering with rage as she surrounded herself with a force field, making even Zap Boy's best shots against her totally useless.

'Fly!' Raffety yelled, grabbing Wham's collar and zooming out of the broken window into the freezing night. But Empress Ogoron wasn't finished yet. Her transformation was almost complete, revealing an armour of long, thick cables that lashed out into the night air, grabbing aimlessly at the nothingness around her, hoping for a strike.

But Zap Boy was too small a target for such a huge monster. Focusing his mind on dodging the swirling cables around him, he held tightly onto Wham and soared up and away until they were finally out of range. Hovering several hundred metres above Kutan World, Zap Boy shuddered at his next thought.

'We've got to go back, Wham,' he gasped, his heart pounding with fear. 'Wonder is still in there and we have to help him.'

'Woof,' barked Wham, already pawing his way back towards the building.

Inside Kutan World, the monster that was the Empress Ogoron let out an almighty wail as she recoiled into the building.

'That power burst must have sapped her energy,' though Raffety, hoping that she wasn't about to transform again – this time into something that could fly.

Zap Boy and Wham flew down to the lower levels and zapped their way in through an air vent. Zooming invisibly around Kutan World, they easily evaded the security guards and soldiers but could find no sign of Wonder.

'Maybe Wonder got away from Spite and headed straight back to our flat,' Zap Boy wheezed after several hours of fruitless hunting. But even as he said it, Zap Boy was aware of a horrible feeling in the pit of his stomach. 'But what if he didn't get away from Spite?' he thought.

Feeling totally exhausted and depressed, Zap Boy and Wham headed for home through an electrical storm that tested their powers of endurance to the limit. They finally got home in the very early hours of the morning.

'Where were you?' Mr Ray exclaimed, stepping into the hall after hearing the door open. 'Your mum's been held for questioning. They caught her with a box full of *your* toys.'

'I had detention,' Raffety mumbled as he stumbled in. 'And then I got into a fight with Konor Kram and...'

Raffety felt himself running out of steam.

'And look at the state of you both!' exclaimed Mr Ray.

Mr Ray ushered Raffety through to the kitchen sink and turned on the taps.

'Listen Raffety, whatever you've been up to tonight, you must know this,' he whispered, his face etched in worry. 'There was an arachnacam in the bath and I couldn't get it down the plughole. It's still in the flat somewhere.'

'I'll find it and squash it,' said Raffety.

'And then they send more,' said Mr Ray, frustrated that his son could be so dumb. 'They're watching us. Step out of line – even a little – and they'll have you down the mines.'

'The mines!' gasped Raffety. His father had never mentioned the mines before.

'Shhh!' Mr Ray hushed, putting his fingers to his lips. For the first time, Raffety wondered if his dad's sudden change of behaviour after his arrest was simply his way of trying to protect the family.

'I'm sorry, son, but I had to shred all your toy designs and homemade comics,' Mr Ray went on, observing what little colour there was in Raffety's face drain away. 'They were great, son,' he added, kindly. 'Let's hope Zap Boy and Wonder really can change the world, eh?' He tried to give Raffety a reassuring wink but it looked like a nervy twitch.

Depressed to find his room tidy and filled with Thought and Learning Control toys, Raffety returned to the kitchen, tossed a frozen snack into the blaster and forked out a tin of beef for Wham. His Dad quickly joined them.

'Dad,' said Raffety. 'They're not going to brainwash Mum, are they?'

Mr Ray looked thoughtful and very stern.

'Your mother is very strong-willed,' he replied. 'She'll be all right. Don't give up.'

'Yeah,' Raffety mumbled, taking out his snack. 'Thanks, Dad.'

'Maybe Dad is all right after all,' he thought.

With no computer in his room, Raffety waited until he heard his dad go to bed and then made his way to the living-room. Outside, the thunder roared as every few seconds another bolt of lightning shook the tower block and disrupted the electrical power. Hacking into the family network and onto the hyperweb, Raffety quickly checked the Zap Boy blog.

'Nearly half a million hits,' he trembled, feeing weak in the knees.

Thinking about tomorrow, Raffety suddenly realized how dangerous it could be for any kid who tried to use a homemade Wonder Zap that didn't work. 'I'll be caught and sent to the coal mines beyond the Wall,' he thought, dropping to his knees in despair. 'I mean, what's the point of the ultimate toy if it doesn't work?'

Raffety Ray lay there for several minutes until a voice in his head said, 'But what if it does? Then what?'

It hit Raffety for the first time that there wasn't actually a plan. 'Ok,' he thought, 'There may be thousands and thousands of kids out there with a groovy new toy, but what are they going to do with it?' And then it came to him. He sat up. 'It might just work,' he mumbled as he started to mull it over. It was a long shot – a one in a billion chance, it seemed right then. But it was still a chance. 'I still have the powers that Wonder gave me,' he told himself. 'And there are thousands of children out there with a Wonder Zap-1. If it does work and we combine our efforts in a coordinated way we could still show Crabwitch – Empress Ogoron – whoever she is, that we mean serious business.'

Raffety quickly wrote his idea onto the Zap Boy blog, signing off just as a huge bolt of lightning ripped through the sky and all the electrical power across London cut out. The computer battery kicked in, but now the screen revealed only reams and reams of computer code against a blue screen.

'It's crashed!' Raffety groaned.

Using his Wonder Zap-1 as a torch, Raffety and Wham went to the bedroom. They sat together, boy and dog, and stared glumly out into the black, smog-filled sky, desperately hoping for a sign of their alien friend.

'Spite must have got to him,' Raffety muttered after a while.

'I've always hated cats,' Wham growled. 'You can never trust them.'

'And Crabwitch isn't going to rest until she's

hunted me down and wiped me out too,' Raffety concluded.

Thinking of all the power Crabwitch could wield against them was overwhelming. It took many hours before Raffety and Wham finally fell to sleep, exhausted, miserable and terrified of what would happen if Raffety's plan didn't work.

A SUPERHERO
IS BORN

The next morning, Raffety awoke in a dark room to the sound of thunder and lightning. With all the power still down, he quickly tried to make contact with Anna Polanski at the Heaps using his Wonder Zap, but the signal cut out too quickly.

'This is hopeless,' he muttered.

He was about to stuff the Wonder Zap-1 into his pocket when his finger accidently hit the number 2 button. In a flash, a video of Geerta Crabwitch's freakish transformation into a Zheta alien was showing on his monitor.

'The Wonder Zap has an inbuilt camera just like any other hand-held computer or phone,' thought Raffety, recalling a function he'd practically ridiculed the day he and Wonder invented it.

Suddenly, Raffety knew that he had everything he needed to bring Crabwitch down.

'I've got to post this on the Zap Boy blog,' he thought, shaking with excitement. 'It will be all over the hyperweb in minutes.'

Raffety's original stunt with Minister Crabwitch's wig had been shut down, quickly followed by false reports that the rebels had faked her freakish appearance. This video, however, left nothing to anyone's imagination.

Raffety knew that the home computer had crashed last night during the storm, so he decided that his best chance was to zap the video over to Anna Polanski at the Heaps. 'She's got so many laptops wired up to old batteries over there she can load this up no problem,' he thought. He tried several times to send the video file direct to Anna's Wonder Zap and a few times thought that it had gone – but he wasn't sure. Realizing it was late and that his dad had already left for work,

Raffety quickly got ready for school and stuffed the Wonder Zap into his pocket.

The electrical storm was slowly giving way to a bitterly cold wind, and by the time Raffety arrived at Barmy Towers to find the holding cage crammed with tired, excitable kids, it was starting to sleet.

'Nine o'clock,' Raffety overheard a Year 8 girl say to her friend as he mingled with the crowd. He listened avidly to the mutterings around him.

'Have you tried it?'

'I got a connection twice.'

'The signal's definitely getting better.'

'But we can't connect to the alien power stream until 9:00 – it's part of Zap Boy's plan.'

Raffety felt a glimmer of hope. 'Word about my plan is definitely spreading,' he thought. 'We just need the cyberlink to Wonder's baseship to last long enough and we can show Crabwitch and Prime Minister Shrub that we really mean business.'

It was then that the power all over London

came back on.

Seconds before the school siren blared, Raffety felt the first drops of snow on his face.

'It's white,' he thought, gazing up in astonishment. 'This could be the first white Christmas in years.'

After their morning tests, all the pupils were marched into assembly with Dr Braincrammer. Everyone's eyes were fixed on the clock above his head.

'... and that is why all of you must cram much harder for this week's tests...' Dr Braincrammer lectured. 'Facts, facts, fact — that's what will make you good citizens...'

'This is it,' thought Raffety. 'If my plan doesn't work, I really am a total washout.'

As children all over the country counted down the seconds to 09:00, Raffety saw many at his school slowly reach for their pockets.

'They are the ones with a Wonder Zap,' he thought, feeling really excited now. He followed the seconds on the clock and counted down. 'Five, four, three, two, one...' The head of nearly every child looked down and then...

NOTHING.

'There's no signal,' Raffety hissed through gritted teeth, when none of the children around him disappeared. It was only when several children screamed and others fainted that Raffety remembered Wonder Zap-1's incredible powers.

'Of course, *we* can still see each other,' he thought. 'But to anyone without a Wonder Zap it looks like half the school have just vanished!'

Seeing nothing in the hall but a scattering of terrified children and a team of bewildered teachers, Dr Braincrammer collapsed into his luxurious chair.

'Let's play!' Raffety shouted.

There was a huge cheer followed by a stampede to the exits. Raffety flew out the door and up into a morning sky filled with a fall of beautiful soft white snow.

'Hey, wait for me!' barked Wham, paddling up from the kerb.

But the excitement lasted only a minute. On what should have been the best day of his life, Raffety Ray felt utterly deflated.

'I wish Wonder was here,' he mumbled to Wham.

Raffety and Wham flew over London watching children everywhere playing in the white snow: making snowmen, chucking snowballs, sliding, skating, tobogganing –

everything that kids played back in the old days before Thought and Learning Control toys and Braincramming had ever been heard of. Visiting the Heaps, they found Anna Polanski alone in the hideout, sitting before her laptop.

'Did you get my message and the video file?' Raffety asked, still deep in thought about Wonder. Anna grinned and gestured to the official news channel she was watching.

'They've removed all hyperweb restrictions so that people all over the country can see this,' Anna garbled, so excited she could hardly sit still. 'Raffety, that video of yours was the best weapon we could ever have had.'

'So the hyperweb is open to everyone,' Raffety was thinking. Absorbing one monumental revelation at a time was the best he could manage.

'People are calling it an alien attack and there's been a massive swing in public opinion against Prime Minister Shrub and the entire government,' Anna went on. 'They're blaming Shrub for being weak — for letting that alien monster take control and for extinguishing every imaginative thought from our minds. It was a brilliant plan.'

'Woof' barked Wham, getting excited.

'Without imagination there are no new ideas to challenge anyone in power,' Anna continued. 'People just accept what they have because they're too stressed out and tired to do anything about it.'

Raffety was still feeling too low to fully grasp what all this actually meant.

'They're saying it's the end of Brain-cramming,' said Anna, trying to state things as clearly as she could, 'that children need toys and time for play. They've even opened the border by the Wall, and Correction Schools and coal mines all over the country are opening their doors.'

Just then, the image of Prime Minister Shrub flashed onto TV screens all over the country.

'If you're out there, Zap Boy, I'm ready to talk,' he started. A large splodgy cake was thrust into Shrub's face by an invisible hand.

'The children have even got into Kutan

Studios,' Anna cheered, clapping her hands with glee. 'This is amazing!'

'I'm begging you, Zap Boy,' the Prime Minister spurted, wiping the raspberry jam from his beard, 'I want to hear your demands. Make yourself known to us now, *please.*'

A big bowl of custard appeared to pour itself over Shrub's head while a sharp yank on his TLC tie jerked him headfirst into a plate of brown blancmange.

Raffety was feeling almost ok.

'Come on, you lot, take a look at this!' panted a young boy, gesturing at the door for everyone to come outside.

Scrambling up to the summit of the highest heap, Raffety, Wham and Anna gazed out over a twinkling city skyline.

'Wow!' sighed Anna. 'It's beautiful!'

'There are Christmas lights on all over the country,' panted the boy. 'They say a mob of children and parents broke into the National Power Station in Kutan and demanded that they re-route power to street lights and homes everywhere.'

'Now Crabwitch isn't siphoning off most of our electricity there'll be enough for all of us,' said Anna.

'Let's hope we stopped her in time,' thought Raffety, thinking of the Zheta battlestar set to attack Uaan-4. 'Then at least Wonder's sacrifice will not have been in vain.'

Anna returned to the hideout to organize supper while Raffety and Wham remained at the summit, privately mourning their friend. Suddenly, Wham saw something that sent him bursting into a volley of wildly enthusiastic barks.

'Calm down, boy,' Raffety urged kindly, 'They're only fireworks.'

The sky was alive with exploding rockets. But then Raffety too saw something that made his heart skip.

'It's a spaceship,' he mumbled, following the bright light heading straight for them.

There was only a handful of children in the Heaps and none of them seemed at all aware of the approaching craft. Raffety felt his heart racing with eager anticipation.

The spaceship swept down and hovered, just metres from where they were standing.

'Wonder!' cried Raffety, overjoyed to see the very happy alien beaming at them through the cockpit window.

Within minutes Zap Boy and Wham had joined Wonder in the spaceship and were looping the loop through the Christmas tree lights all over London, where thousands of parents and children

had come out to watch the evening's stunning events.

'Look at all the graffiti slogans,' Raffety cheered.

'But Wonder, how did you get away from Spite?' asked Raffety.

Wonder grinned. 'Wonder has less strength than Empress Ogoron's cat but far more brain power and skill. I detected Empress Ogoron's spaceship on my sensors and took it before she could get away.'

'You *stole* Empress Ogoron's spaceship!' Raffety cried with joy.

'Now she has to hide,' said Wonder. 'There's no way home for her without it.'

'She'll head for the land beyond the Wall,' said Raffety. 'The police will never find her there — there's no surveillance, no electricity grid — nothing.'

'And without electricity she will fade away,' said Wonder. 'Even now the Zheta battlestar is in retreat.'

'Good riddance,' yapped Wham.

Raffety wondered what an alien like Empress Ogoron, stranded on Earth without her spaceship, might yet do to regain her strength. But for now at least, they were safe. 'With Crabwitch gone children everywhere will be free to play and it's all thanks to you!' Raffety felt a lump come to his throat.

Wonder shook his head.

'We did it together,' he said firmly.

But Raffety knew also that with this spaceship Wonder would soon be heading home.

'Wonder,' he said cautiously, 'What will happen to our powers after you've gone?'

Wonder looked affectionately at his Earthling friends.

'I have given you and Wham the powers of the Uaan race,' he said with a wry smile. 'And I trust you both to use them well in the future. But after tonight, no more Wonder Zap powers for anyone. Too much power isn't good for anyone – not even children.'

Raffety laughed. He understood exactly what Wonder meant. He took Wonder's hand and gave it a firm shake.

'I'll never forget you, Wonder,' he said.

Wonder found a quiet place at the Heaps to drop Raffety and Wham at around 22:15 and. Raffety sent Anna a message to join them to say a final farewell to their alien friend. Before long they were both waving goodbye and Wham was excitedly barking his own send-off message. As the spaceship disappeared from view, Raffety felt a strange mixture of sadness, pride and great excitement.

'Just imagine what we could all do now,' he said to his friends.

As they walked back towards the hideout Raffety sent his dad a text on his Wonder Zap-1. His dad texted right back to say that his mum had returned from the police station and that they were searching the streets, trying to find him.

'I'm meeting my mum and dad back at the estate,' Raffety told Anna. He took a good look at his dear, dear friend. 'Would you like to come. We have a spare room.'

Anna smiled. 'My home is here for now,' she

smiled. 'But you must promise to come back and see us all soon.'

Many of Anna's gang had worked together to prepare hot chocolate for everyone but Raffety just wanted to get home.

'Wham needs a decent meal,' Raffety explained. He gave Wham a grin and ruffled his head. 'A big tin of beef.'

'Good boy.' Wham yapped, wagging his tail.

Raffety found his mum and dad waiting anxiously by the bins outside the entrance to Tower Block 23.

'Oh Raffety,' his mum smiled tearfully, giving him a long hug. 'Have you heard the news? Crabwitch is an alien. The police are trying to find her, but she's disappeared.'

'All right, son?' said Mr Ray, giving his son a pat on the back. 'I suppose you got yourself one of those wonderful doodle-flip-thing-ees,' he added sheepishly. 'I'd love to see one.'

Raffety recognized the playful glint in his father's eye.

'No worries, dad,' he said with a smile.

For the first time in years, the lights in Tower Block 23 were blazing. The Ray family reached the third-floor landing to find a miserable Sky Chang lurking there.

'You should be out having fun, Sky,' said Mrs Ray cheerfully. 'Haven't you got one of those Wonder Zaps?'

Sky lowered her head.

'Shame,' said Mrs Ray.

Raffety and his parents went straight to the kitchen, and while Raffety got Wham his well-earned bowl of beef, Mr Ray did something truly amazing. He cooked.

'Who fancies bubble and squeak?' he asked, pulling the Christmas leftovers out of the fridge.

'So what now?' asked Mrs Ray as they dug in to their midnight meal. 'The Prime Minister wants to meet with this Zap Boy and hear his demands. Do you think that Zap Boy will actually reveal himself and go?'

'But what if Zap Boy isn't ready to show his true identify to the world?' replied Raffety.

His parents looked thoughtful for a moment.

'Well... I think Zap Boy, whoever he is, will always do the right thing,' said Dad.

'For all of us,' said Mum. 'Wherever we are. Whenever we need him.'

Raffety nodded, slowly.

'What do you think, Raffety?' asked Dad.

Raffety had already decided that he would use his powers to keep his identity hidden while he made his demands to President Shrub.

'You know, I think you're both right,' he replied with a grin.

ABOUT THE WRITER

Adam Guillain was born into a family-run theatre school. He became a holiday-camp bluecoat before turning his hand to sports journalism, music and then teaching. After throwing it all in to live in a tropical rainforest and work with Zanzibari teachers and children for two years, he took up novel writing. Adam is the author of many picture books and novels for children including the *Bella Balistica* series, *Ghoul School* and *Our Neighbour's a Vampire*. In 2005, Adam was appointed writer in residence at the Roald Dahl Museum and Story Centre in Great Missenden and in 2007 joined The Story Museum team in Oxford, combining his writing with storytelling performances, author visits and teaching 'Story into Creative Writing' to children, parents and teachers all over the country.

www.adam-guillain.co.uk